FRANKENLOUSE

Mary James
also known as M.E. Kerr

SCHOLASTIC HARDCOVER

Scholastic Inc. New York

Library of Congress Cataloging-in-Publication Data
James, Mary
Frankenlouse / by Mary James.
p.   cm.
Summary: Fourteen-year-old Nick finds life dreary at the military
academy run by his strict father and dreams of becoming a cartoonist.
ISBN 0-590-46528-7
[1. Schools — Fiction. 2. Cartoons and comics — Fiction.
3. Fathers and sons — Fiction.] I. Title.
PZ7.J15417Fr   1994
[Fic] — dc20   93-39651
                                                              CIP
                                                               AC

12 11 10 9 8 7 6 5 4 3 2 1   4 5 6 7 8 9/9

Printed in the U.S.A.   37

First Scholastic printing, November 1994

For Bill Van Assen

CHAPTER ONE

The Little Soldiers were marching. We called them worms.

Not a one was over five feet.

They wore light blue pants with red stripes down the sides, navy blue jackets with brass buttons, white garrison belts, and white visor caps.

They were billeted in Slaughter, a gray house in the circle of barracks and buildings that surround the large concrete square known as The Yard.

Last year I was one of them, but Slaughter wasn't my billet.

I've always lived in the large, white colonial house on the hill, the residence of General Patch Reber.

A West Point graduate, and a veteran of Vietnam, he is the commanding officer of Blister Mil-

itary Academy. He is the designer of the Blister
logo, which somehow ended up to look like

B   M
A

. . . earning the academy the nickname BAM.

My father is a control freak.

He's as hidden as BAM is with its high, ivy-
covered walls. His hair is black, his eyes are
technicolor blue. He has a bone-chilling stare
which would soon be directed at the 150 cadets
enrolled for that academic year.

He's my father, but I'm not named for him.
Blister men don't have juniors.

The Little Soldiers chanted as they marched.

We're marching smart,
Left right left right,
We take the flag down
Every night!
We're worms right now,
And so it goes,
But someday we'll
Be Blister crows!

Everything stops for "Retreat."

Even I did. I put my pencil down, stood up, and placed my hand over my heart.

Everyone at Blister was doing the same thing, including the senior "crows" who couldn't see The Yard from their barracks.

Even Ike, our dog, got to his feet and wagged his tail.

Bugles blared out from loudspeakers all over Blister.

I am called Nick.

I was fourteen the year of this story, the year that changed my life.

A story about me is one about my father, too, as surely as a story about Old Dominion, Virginia, is about Blister Military Academy, which looms over that village like an apparition.

CHAPTER TWO

There was always tension in our house near six in the evening.

My grandfather shuffled into the living room at ten to, and asked me what I was drawing.

I was working on my idea for a cartoon strip. I'd invented a world of these teeny insects who live in books — you see them sometimes crawling down the page like tiny dots the size of a pin's head. They're book lice.

My strip concerned a louse who lived in *Frankenstein*. He really belonged in a horror library but his owner had lent him out before he ever got there, so that he ended up among books of poetry, music, art, and literature.

One of my father's favorite sayings was "You are where you came from." It was usually accompanied by "Blood will tell," meaning your background will give you away.

In my cartoon world, these lice took after the book they lived in. Frankenlouse is a monster and all the lice in this library fear him. Their dialogue bubbles call out reports on him, and warnings concerning his ways.

I didn't tell my grandfather this.

I told him I was sketching Caleb Purr, who was on report for insubordination, and as punishment was raking leaves in our yard.

Caleb's father was Peter Purr, the famous weatherman from *The Good Morning Show* and *After Dark*.

I did have one sketch of Caleb. I showed it to my grandfather.

He said, "I saw his father on TV the other night." He looked at his watch. He was carrying a Scotch and soda.

I imitated Caleb's father's trademark: "This is Peter Purr, and I'll be purrin' atcha!"

My grandfather snorted. He said, "We get 'em all, don't we? All the sons of famous fathers, and now we got *her*."

He meant Jessie Southgate, our fifth female cadet. She was twelve, which made her a Little Soldier. But if I'd glanced out the window to see them break from "Retreat," I wouldn't have been able to tell which cadet she was. Females wore the same Blister uniform. They tucked their hair up under their caps.

Jessie's mom was Unique Southgate. Unique never used a last name. She was like Madonna or Cher, and she was on MTV like they were. She'd made movies, too, mostly X-rated ones.

All of BAM knew who Jessie was. But the press didn't know she was enrolled at Blister, and my father wanted to keep it that way.

I looked at my watch, too.

It was almost time for him to come barging through the door.

Our housekeeper, Fanny, was in the kitchen with the cook. She was probably eyeing the kitchen clock. She was making sure dinner would be ready on time. . . . If it wasn't, The General would explode.

We ate on the dot of six. Or at 1800 hours, as my father put it.

My grandfather, Stone Reber, padded about in his moccasins checking the time again.

All Reber males have black hair and blue eyes. His hair had silver in it. He was an old soldier, a West Pointer, too. Sometimes he called The Point "Woo Poo."

He was a World War II veteran.

Our dog headed for the door. He had built-in

time. He knew that in a few minutes my father would appear. Ike sat there waiting.

My grandfather wore khaki pants and a khaki shirt. He put on a striped tie every night at this time because my father wouldn't sit down at the table with a tieless male.

Grandad once wanted to be a poet. He went to Woo Poo instead, where he read and memorized all the poems he spouted on special occasions: birthdays, Christmas, Thanksgiving, etcetera.

His favorite poet was Henry Wadsworth Longfellow.

In my cartoon world there was a louse who lived in Longfellow's collected works. He always spoke in rhyme.

I wanted to be an artist since I was old enough to hold onto a pencil. One of my favorite artists was an ex-Marine named George Booth. He was famous for the animals he drew, wild-looking cats with frizzled whiskers and a grumpy-looking English bull terrier.

Once I showed my father a Booth cartoon.

It didn't knock his socks off.

Cartooning wasn't a profession in his eyes. It was a waste of time. Sketching was okay and not okay. I sketched all the time and it was okay when he was in a good mood, and not when he

wasn't. But trying to make anything like a cartoon strip from my sketches would have been a
red blinker light of warning to him. It would
warn: WATCH OUT! It would bring mental pictures to his mind of a future in which I would
not choose to go to The Point. It would threaten
him, and if he knew I had such an idea in my
head he would stamp it out like someone beating
away at a brushfire until there was only charred
remains and dying smoke.

Ike was on his feet.

Grandfather was taking a last swallow of his
drink.

Fanny had come out of the kitchen.

The old clock in the tower bonged ONE . . .
TWO . . . THREE, and on FOUR the front door
opened.

My father was home at two minutes to six.

> FRANKENLOUSE IS IN THE HOUSE!

> A MENTAL LOUSE IS IN THE HOUSE!

CHAPTER THREE

Last year on spring break, when my parents were still together, my father took us on a camping trip at Lake Leary, in Georgia, a boyhood haunt of his.

I was sitting on the dock, fishing, my pole hanging in the water, while I thought about a cartoon featuring a gentleman carrying a pair of hands into a hand laundry.

Suddenly my father shouted: "Nick! Don't move!"

I froze.

Behind me, my father kicked a long, ugly-looking black snake off the dock, where it was poised to strike at me.

I watched it flip into the water.

I heard my mother shout, "Oh, thank heaven you didn't move, Nick!"

Move?

It would never have occurred to me to disobey an order.

I am a child of discipline.

The snake was a poisonous sidewinder, and I would have been dead if I had not been Patch Reber's son.

CHAPTER
FOUR

"What are you drawing Caleb for?" my father asked after dinner.

He had picked up my sketchbook, open to the drawing of Caleb in our front yard.

My heart skipped a beat. I was afraid he'd flip through the rest of it and see Frankenlouse wearing his celluloid eyeshield, crawling from the bookcase toward Longfellow.

All monster lice liked to eat the letters from the words other lice lived on. Since Frankenlouse was the only monster louse in this particular library, he could eat all he wanted for he had no competition. He had no friends, either, so he ate, ate, ate, earning the reputation of a hungry and horrible creature.

Longfellow lived on the sentence *From the waterfall he named her, Minnehaha, Laughing Water.*

Frankenlouse had already made quite a dent

in Longfellow's address, which now read: *From
    waterfall e named er, Minne a a, Laug ing
Water.*

"I drew Caleb because he was there," I told
my father.

That was his kind of logic. Straight ahead. Men
climb mountains because they're there. *A* follows
B. One follows two. Night follows day.

My father never removed his tie until he put
on his pajamas. Once I did a sketch of him crawling into bed in the white BAM pajamas, with a
necktie on.

"Three days into the first semester and Caleb
is already on report," my father grumbled.

Caleb was drawn to trouble like a moth to
the flame. Caleb was fourteen, too. He'd nor-
mally be billeted in the barracks. But at com-
mencement last year he'd managed to drop
a whole bottle of Bromo Seltzer in the water
carafe on the dais a moment before the pro-
gram began. As my father welcomed parents to
Blister, the water rose, pushed through the lid
and began flowing down on my father's prepared
speech.

That earned Caleb another year in Slaughter.

The other thing Caleb was drawn to was
skateboarding.

My father said, "I never met a skateboarder I really liked."

Caleb is Captain of Blister's Yard Bombers.

"How many have you met, sir?"

"Enough. It's *where* they skate, maybe. Behind the gym here, and in town they skate in back alleys, and back behind the 7-Eleven."

I was waiting for him to start turning the pages of my sketchbook, waiting for that look he'd get on his face when he saw something that upset the perfect order of his life . . . like the day he came home and found a large trunk on the floor in my mother's room.

But he simply said, "I doubt that Caleb will ever be a crow," and he put the sketchbook down. (Thank God!)

Seniors were called "crows" because of the black capes they were issued in their last year at BAM.

"You waste too much time drawing, Nick," my father said.

"Yes, sir." It was always easier to agree with him, unless you had no plans for the following hour.

He sat down in his favorite armchair, the big, comfortable leather one no one was allowed to sit in but him.

Ike got up there sometimes. Ike was a long-haired, black dachshund, and often my father found a dark hair on the chair and started yelling at Ike, "Did *you* do this?"

Ike would run for cover, tail between his legs, nose pointed straight ahead.

My father put on this old celluloid eyeshade he wore when he read. He liked to read books about the military. But first, every evening after dinner, he read two newspapers: *The Wall Street Journal* and *The New York Times*.

Without my mother there, the house was as tidy and quiet as a barracks room during class time. My grandfather was looser in attitude than my father, but they were both Army men who were unlikely to play music or kick off their shoes as they sat around, or leave open magazines across chairs, or apple cores in saucers on tabletops.

I did my homework on the couch across from my father. *Write a composition about a family.* The minute Lieutenant Meadow assigned it, hands shot up. Whose family? She said, "That's up to you." An imaginary family or a real family? She said, "That's up to you." A whole family or someone in a family? She said, "That's up to you." On and on. It was a trick. Lieutenant

Meadow hoped to learn more about the new cadets in English 1.

I was stuck. I couldn't write about my mother, the only interesting member of our family. My father had warned me that I was not to wash our dirty linen in public.

Was I supposed to coax snores out of Lieutenant Meadow with the exciting revelation that both my grandfather and my father were named after Generals Stone and Patch?

My father said, "Nick, you're jiggling your knee."

"Sorry, sir."

"What are you working on?"

"I'm not working on anything yet. I'm blocked."

"Blocked?" My father said it in the tone of voice he might use if he were asking "Robbed?" "Defeated?" "Ambushed?" It was unfathomable to him — this idea of being blocked.

I told him about the assignment, and that it was hard to think of anything.

He said, "Leave your mother out of it."

"I know that."

"It might be interesting to write about the fact that both your grandfather and I were named after famous generals."

"That's an idea," I said.

Then he returned to his newspaper.

Five minutes later he said, "Nick, you're humming."

"I am?"

Humming and drumming your fingers."

"Sorry, sir."

I finally went up to my room to jiggle my knee, hum, and drum until an idea came to me.

My grandfather had gone for a walk, taking Ike with him. He was a smoker in a smoke-free environment, an issue which was argued back and forth between my father and him when he moved in last August.

He smoked while he walked Ike. During the day he sneaked smokes, then sprayed the house with Glade air freshener.

His room was my mother's sewing room. My mother never sewed anything, but that was my father's name for it, anyway. That was what he imagined a woman did in a room she took as her own. She'd paid bills in there, written letters, and ridden an exercise bike. She'd had a small RCA TV in there, too, which my grandfather used now to watch old movies late at night. She'd also painted in there, sometimes, or made collages. I suppose that's where my own interest in art came from. . . . The Patch side of the family thought Art was a nickname for Arthur.

Fanny was upstairs turning down my father's bed.

My father liked clean pajamas every day, laid out on the top blanket, with a Kleenex containing a multivitamin, an aspirin, a blood pressure pill, and extra vitamin C. He took them into the bathroom at bedtime, and swallowed them down after he used the Water Pik. Then he gargled very loudly with Listerine.

I sat on my bed and tried to think some more about the composition.

I thought of Frankenlouse, instead. I needed some female lice, or one, maybe, who might be the only character unafraid of Frankenlouse.

By the time taps sounded, I had entered all the dialogue from Frankenlouse in my little Mac, but I had no idea for the English assignment.

Taps sounded at eleven o'clock on the dot. It was my favorite part of any day. Three buglers played it from far ends of The Yard, answering each other. One went first, then the other, then the last so that you heard taps three times.

Loud first, then softer, and the third bugler, muted.

I missed my mother most then.

* * *

When the phone rang near midnight, I knew
it was trouble of some kind.

I sneaked sleepy-eyed out into the hall, leaned
over the banister and tried to guess what was
up, from my father's end of the conversation.

I heard him bark, "No, I'm not coming down
there! She's not thinking straight!"

A pause.

Then, "Yes, yes, I'm aware it will be in all the
newspapers! But if I come down there now it
will be a dead giveaway there is some connection
between her and BAM!"

Another pause.

Finally, "She would not want that! Good
night!"

I went downstairs. My father was pacing.

"Sir?"

"What are you doing out of bed, Nick?"

"The phone."

"What *about* the phone?"

"Is something wrong?" I wanted to add "with
Mother" but I knew better.

My father pointed to the staircase I had just
come down.

"Go!" he said. "On the double!"

"My God!" I muttered. "This place!" I muttered.

"And don't sleep in your underwear! What do you think your pajamas are for?"

I kept going, kept muttering.

"Did you *hear* me, Nick? Put on pajamas!"

"Yes, sir!"

CHAPTER FIVE

My father always said she ran off.

It made my mother sound like some dog who had wandered away, maybe with a piece of rope still attached to its collar, as though it had tugged on it until it snapped and gave it freedom it didn't know what to do with, anyway. You imagine it running wild, panting, down back roads and through bad weather, hungry and lost.

Actually her trunk was open for weeks in the sewing room as she packed.

In a lot of ways she prepared me for it.

She never said that one day she would send for me after she got to New York City. She said, instead, that I was going to make a good crow, that there was plenty of time to think about what I would do after that.

I remember the day she said all this she knelt

down and put her arms around me. She smelled of Charlie, a perfume she liked and I would buy her for Christmas or her birthday. Her long blonde hair was falling out of the combs she used to keep it back. She was wearing jeans and an old Metallica T-shirt. She went barefoot every chance she got — that used to bug my father — and that day she was barefoot, too. She was playing that old Bruce Springsteen album *Human Touch*. We'd been picking some of the horror/fantasy books she liked out of her bookshelf for her to take: Stephen King and Harlan Ellison and Jane Yolen, and she handed me *Frankenstein* that day and said, "Ever read it?"

"I saw the movie."

"No, this is the original. Take it, Nick. You'll like it."

She said that I would always have her address and her phone number, and that I could contact her anytime. *But*, she said, she hoped that in the new semester I would concentrate on my studies, and make it as easy as possible on my father.

"Are you leaving him for another man?" I asked her.

"No. Absolutely not."

"Then what's going on?" I asked her.

"*I* am," she answered. "*I'm* going on. I have

to do this, Nicky. I can't explain it to you so you'll understand, but I've put this off and put it off, and now you're not a worm anymore, you're a big guy.

"Every night at eleven — when taps sounds? I'll think of you, Nick. I've always loved that sweet time when those cadet horns wail at each other that way. It's something about BAM I'll really miss."

One night when I was leaning over the banister listening to my father talk about it with my grandfather, I heard him say, "She's probably run off with someone she met on one of her trips to New York."

"That's not like Terri," said my grandfather.

"There's no other reason a woman just runs off," said my father.

He was a linear thinker.

Everything went in a line.

Everything had one dimension.

CHAPTER SIX

"Nick?" Caleb called to me after gym, "Wait up!"

Caleb was tall and blond, with a long nose and not much chin. He'd sit in classes with his elbow resting on the desk, and his left hand covering his chin. He'd sit there doodling skateboards and dreaming up trouble, like the time he put a cup of sugar down the gas tank of Captain Tuttle's Pinto, just as Tuttle thought he was off for a long weekend with skis strapped to the roof of his car.

"Did you hear what happened last night?" Caleb walked into the locker room with me. "Unique got arrested. There was a riot outside Roanoke after a rock concert and she socked a cop. They say she's right downtown in the slammer."

"Who says?"

"It was on the radio."

Worms are not supposed to have radios, but Caleb had always kept a small Sony Walkman in his room behind his books.

I thought of my father's midnight phone call as I listened to Caleb tell me more details.

I thought of my father saying, "If I come down there now it will be a dead giveaway that there is some connection between her and BAM." And I thought of him telling me once about Unique's fear that Jessie could be kidnapped, somehow, if it got around that she was enrolled with us.

That very minute Jessie Southgate was changing from her gymsuit to her school clothes in the faculty bathroom down the hall. BAM still didn't have all the facilities needed for female cadets.

"Who bailed her out?" I asked Caleb. That was probably what my father was supposed to have done.

"How do I know? Some lucky ass."

"Does Jessie know?"

"Who knows what she knows? She's this little mouse, Nick. She doesn't say two words. But it'll be in all the newspapers."

Caleb had one of those wash-off tattoos on his behind. The words TAKE A RIDE were drawn on a skateboard. "I think Jessie chills out or something. You can tell her you saw Unique dancing in nothing but her undies and boots on MTV and she just looks right through you."

"Maybe it won't make the papers."

"Are you kidding? Remember when my old man got a facelift? He thought the reporters would buy the idea he was in the hospital for a checkup and a month later *Spy* magazine ran before-and-after pictures."

We headed for the showers. I said, "Why'd he get a facelift? He's only about forty isn't he?"

"Forty-one. He wants to act. That's what he's always wanted. He doesn't know zilch about weather! That's why I'm never mentioned in his publicity. I make him look old."

We turned on the faucets and kept talking while we soaped up. "Forty-one's not that old," I said. "My own mother is thirty-nine."

Caleb shouted above the steam. "My old man says forty-one's not old until you're forty-one. . . . He had bags." I could see Caleb pull the skin out under one eye. Then he gave himself a mock punch under his chin. "This was getting double."

He soaped his butt and said, "Damn! I forgot!"

His tattoo was bleeding.

Caleb was busy fixing a new tattoo on himself. I didn't wait for him because he started trying to sell me on joining The Yard Bombers.

Mostly worms were Bombers. Skateboarding hadn't caught on with the upperclassmen yet.

I didn't want to hang out with worms, even though I liked Caleb the best of anyone at BAM, and technically he wasn't a Little Soldier, he only lived at Slaughter as punishment. One worm from Slaughter, okay, but two or three for friends looked like you couldn't move on.

The Little Soldier image was hard to lose at BAM. For years you were this worm all the grown-up civilians wanted to coo at, and lift up like you were a doll or a dog. The upperclassmen wiggled their first fingers at you when they saw you. The crows pitied you, you knew they did because they winked at you or handed you candy bars like soldiers in a foreign land winning over the kiddies.

Caleb passed me a skateboarding magazine he got an upperclassmen to buy for him in Old Dominion. He said to just look it over, and I slapped it into my briefcase.

My hair was still wet, combed back, and dripping. I started down the basement hall just as she came out of the faculty john.

"Hi, Jessie!"

"Do I know you?" She had her cap tucked into her garrison belt, and she was pinning her blonde hair up as she went along.

She was little for twelve. She had green eyes that didn't look at you, and she was in a hurry. We were always in a hurry between classes. They didn't give you that much time. That much time like idle hands are the devil's playmates. You might upset the routine. You might sit down in The Yard and blow the whole Blister look of order and desolation.

I tried to get in step with her. I said, "I'm Nick Reber."

"So?" I thought of her mother dancing with a skeleton on the top of a drum in "Freeborn Woman." A light show blasting above her, guitars screaming, drumbeats. I thought of that eyebrow raised, the top hat over the other eye, the cool look on her face like, I know who *I* am. I couldn't help smiling at little Jessie looking up with an expression that asked, "Who am I?"

Nothing about her said she was her mother's daughter.

"So, I'm glad to meet you," I said.

She said, "Why?"

She might just as well have added, "Because of my mother?"

I said, "It's just an expression. How are you, I'm glad to meet you. It's stuff you say, isn't it?"

She shrugged. She had her hair pinned up

and she put her cap on. We were walking fast. She was looking at her watch.

"How do you like it here?" More stuff you say.

"I've only been here three days. How do you like it here?"

"I've only been here fourteen years."

She gave me a look. Her eyes almost met mine.

I said, "I'm General Reber's son, but don't hold it against me. It's an accident of birth."

"I know what you mean."

Then for the first time her voice changed from flat to upbeat. "You must know everyone! Do you know Caleb Purr?"

"He's my buddy."

"Are you *sure*?" she said, "because I have a note for him. Could you give him this note?" She was getting it out of her pocket. "I won't see him."

"You live at Slaughter, too. How can you not see him?"

"Would you just give him this, please? I have to go to dance class."

"You'll see him before I see him, Jessie."

"I don't want to give it to him. Will you give it to him?"

"Okay." I took it. It was stapled closed. I said, "Have you met Aaron Bindle yet?"

"Who's Aaron Bindle?"

Good question. Who *was* he? No one at Blister really knew Aaron.

I said, "He's a crow. His dad was with the American Ballet."

"His dad was France Bindle?"

"Right. And Aaron's our ballet boy. He dances on his toes in the big Christmas show every year."

"In *The Nutcracker*?"

"Yes. My mother danced the Sugarplum Fairy one year."

"I did, too, in my old school."

"Aaron is mute," I said.

"How does he dance if he's deaf?"

"He's not deaf. He's mute. He never talks."

"*Never?*"

"He can't. You'll see."

The bell rang.

Everyone at BAM was at the mercy of bells, and bugles.

A cadet had just five minutes to get where he was going now or he would walk a punishment tour in The Yard.

We started to jog.

I wondered if Jessie knew about her mother yet.

Walking toward us was Caleb's nemesis, Cap-

tain Tuttle, world class nose picker, an officer
whose morning breath lasted all day long.

At term end, when the yearbook featured
everyone's "faculty buddy," no one wanted
Tuttle.

Twice, my father ordered me to list him as
mine.

This sacrifice on my part did nothing to endear
me to him. Tuttle was not won over easily. People who smell like Tuttle are strangers to kind-
ness. It makes them suspicious.

And anyway, Tuttle was drunk with power in
a little school where he towered over everyone
under his command. His eyes were always
mean, but even meaner as he saw what had
fallen out of my briefcase.

A magazine!

His eyes beamed down on it as though it were
a gun, a knife, a wad of heroin.

Magazines belonged in your room, in your
duffel bag where you kept any allowable traces
of civilian life. One outfit of civilian clothing and
only one. One bar of candy and only one. One
framed photograph for display from six P.M. to
six A.M. and only one. One etcetera and only
one.

Although I lived off-limits, I was still subject
to the same rules when I was on-limits.

"Just a minute, Cadet Reber," said he sharply.

I knew that somewhere in the very near future I would walk one punishment tour . . . and maybe not only one.

Wisely, Jessie Southgate double-timed away from me.

I was a heartbeat from some grotesque fate at the hands of Dragonbreath, and Jessie was on her way to meet Blister's Man of Mystery: Aaron Bindle, who looked right through you when he saw you at all, and the rare times he wanted to tell you something, had his talking machine speak in its robot voice.

It called me Ick.

CHAPTER SEVEN

My father was home at four-thirty that day. I saw his white Jeep in the driveway with the anxiety people in Kansas feel as they view a dark funnel in the sky above.

When I entered the house, Fanny was waiting for me.

"Dinner at five tonight, Nicky," she said.

"How come?"

She raised her hands as though she'd just been ordered to "stick 'em up" and shook her gray head. "Ask your father. I don't know why."

He was nowhere in sight.

I put down my briefcase and petted Ike, who came out from under a chair. Ike knew the timing was way off, and his tail was between his legs as though he was afraid he was to blame, somehow, for my father's being home at that hour.

I could see my grandfather out on the side porch, smoking.

Then I saw the magazine that had fallen out of my briefcase earlier that afternoon. It was resting on the coffee table in our living room.

It was called *Thrasher*.

There was a kid on the cover doing a trick on a skateboard. The cover also promised an interview inside with someone named Jesus Lizard.

I flipped through the pages.

More pictures of skateboarders. Advertisements for Zero T All Vegetarian Shoes, MADD Mike's Bitchin' Boards, and a heavy metal band called Soul Asylum.

Ad slogans bragged "High Fashion For Low Lifes," and promised to "Kick-start your system with the new release from Sex and Suicide."

"Hot Shots" talked about skating with words I usually read on latrine walls in the Old Dominion bus station.

Before I saw more, I heard my father coming downstairs. He was clearing his throat the way he does before a major tirade. That didn't surprise me, considering what I was holding in my hands. What did surprise me was what he had on. He was in full uniform, carrying his braided cap. His twelve embroidered ribbons were arranged across the breast of his jacket in seven rows. He was clean-shaven and smelling of Crabtree & Evelyn face lotion.

He was not smiling.

"Where did it come from?" he asked me, as I put *Thrasher* back on the coffee table.

Ike scooted back under the chair.

"I don't know, sir."

"Captain Tuttle has you on Report."

"I am not surprised, sir."

"Who gave it to you?"

"No one did. I found it in the locker room."

"Who left it there?"

"I have no idea, sir." I still had Jessie's note to Caleb in my pocket.

My father was eyeball-to-eyeball with me.

"Who was in the locker room with you?"

"Everyone from gym."

"All right, Nick. I *know* who you are protecting."

"I'm not protecting anyone, sir."

"Don't lie to me."

"I'm not, sir," but he knew I must lie or squeal, and it was a toss-up *which* he would rather a son of his do.

"All right, Nick. Starting tomorrow morning, *early*," he barked, "you will begin walking a punishment tour in The Yard, until the owner of this magazine comes forward."

"Yes, sir."

"Every free hour you have."

"Yes, sir."

"A magazine like *that*," he grumbled.

"Yes, sir."

"I would not let Ike do his duty on a magazine like that!"

"Yes, sir."

Then he said, "We are eating at five. Someone is expected at six."

This was not a time to say, "Who, sir?"

This was a time to wait for my stomach to stop turning over and my pulse to slow up.

"Fanny?" he shouted. "You may serve!"

My grandfather appeared from outside, giving his mouth a quick spray with a small cylinder of FreshBreath.

We entered the dining room.

After Fanny had put down the mashed potatoes, meat loaf, and vegetable, Grandad ventured, "What's all the mystery?"

"You'll see in time."

"Not Terri?" my grandfather said hopefully.

My father shot him a look.

I sat there chewing my food, remembering not to duck for it or I'd be fined one dollar. There was no way Caleb was going to come forward and claim *Thrasher* as his property. I would be

walking punishment in The Yard everyday until
I was old enough to be a crow.

My food didn't taste good since my stomach
refused to stop doing loops.

My grandfather said, "What *is* this?" He was
holding a piece of okra at the end of his fork.
He said, "This is okra!"

"Yes," my father agreed.

"*Ok-ra!*" my grandfather slid the vegetable off
his fork. "It has slime all over it."

My father said nothing.

"I cannot eat it!"

"Don't eat it," my father suggested.

"Who can eat it?"

"I can eat it," said my father. "Nick can eat
it."

"I can't eat it, sir," I said.

My father said, "*Eat* it!"

"It's the one thing I can't look at or eat!" said
my grandfather.

"Don't eat it."

"I won't. . . . I'm surprised at Fanny."

My father said, "I like it."

"How can you like it?" my grandfather said.
"Don't eat it."

That was about all that was said at that meal.
It was a fast meal, over at five-thirty, after a

dish of Häagen-Dazs chocolate yogurt which Fanny served rather than ice cream, because of my father's cholesterol.

At five-thirty-two Ike started barking.

I looked out the window and saw a long white stretch limo.

"Migawd!" I said. "Who is this?"

My father was reaching for his hat. "This is top secret, Dad, and Nick. Not a word about this!"

She was getting out of the backseat, the chauffeur holding open the door. She was all in white, with high *high* heels, carrying a Siamese cat in her arms.

My mouth fell open, my eyes bulged.

"Unique!" I said. "It's Unique!"

Even my grandfather knew who she was. Who didn't in the whole United States of America, Europe, Asia, etcetera?

"Not her *here*?" my grandfather said.

"Her here," I croaked.

My father said, "I will explain to her that I am going down to Slaughter to get Jessie and bring her back here. . . . You entertain her while I am gone, Dad, Nick. I'll be back ASAP."

My grandfather started upstairs. "I have to gargle before I do anything. I have to get the taste of okra out of my mouth. My mouth tastes putrid!"

My father said, "When I return with Jessie, we'll leave them alone. You'll both go to your rooms."

"I'm your father, remember? Don't order me around," said my grandfather, on the staircase. "Don't tell me to go to my room! I'm going there, anyway, as it happens, but I am not going there because you told me to go there!"

"Just cooperate, *please*. This situation requires discretion and cooperation."

So I was alone with Unique.

I was standing in my living room, and she was sitting on our couch, setting the Siamese cat down on the floor.

Ike liked the cat.

The cat and Ike began to chase around the room.

Unique took a large gold watch off her wrist and put it on the table. It was shaped like a cuff. There was something engraved on it.

She picked up *Thrasher*.

She flipped through it while I read the engraved words: WATCH WHERE YOU GO WITHOUT ME.

"Is this your magazine?" she asked me.

I said, "I found it."

Unique laughed and looked at me with the famous raised eyebrow.

She said, "What a hoot!"

CHAPTER EIGHT

I went to my room immediately when Jessie Southgate arrived at our house with my father, but I did not stay there.

My father took a walk with my grandfather, minus Ike who was intrigued with Unique's cat, Poison.

Poison wore a perfume called that, Unique had told me during the awkward period we were alone together. Poison was Jessie's cat, she said, but she was keeping her for Jessie.

I had stumbled and mumbled my way through the interlude, getting her autograph on my notebook which I took out of my briefcase, asking her what famous rock stars were like, knowing she knew them all.

And she had answered this one was a doll, that one was a pain in the butt (she cleaned up her language for me, I suspect) and she spent a good deal of time talking to Poison, saying things like how does you like dat hairy li'l hot dog, Poisy? Does him scare you, Poisy? Eeew, Poisy, him wants to kiss you, Poisy.

Then I was at my post, the banister, leaning over to listen.

Jessie was sitting on the couch in her uniform, her hands in her lap, a big gift-wrapped box on top of *Thrasher* on the table.

Unique was pacing around in her stiletto heels, babbling away about how brutal the police were, how she was going to sic her lawyers on the Old Dominion police force, how the fight started because the police moved in on the crowd just because they felt like bashing some heads together — her fans were *not* out of line.

"*You* know my fans, honey, they're enthusiastic but they're not violent. They're not like heavy metal audiences. They dance in the aisles, sure, but what kids don't? That's what it's all about!"

Jessie said, "You know who's here? The son of France Bindle. His name is Aaron. I have dance class with him."

"Who's France Bindle, love?"

"He was with the American Ballet."

"I thought you said his name was Aaron."

"That's his son."

"Honey, open your present. I can't stay."

Jessie began to undo the ribbon.

"I got it in Richmond for you, Jess. It looked at me and screamed, 'Take me to Jessie!' "

"What is it, Mother?"

"You'll see. Just tear the paper, love. I have a plane to catch."

Jessie ripped the wrapping from the box.

"If I didn't love you so much, I'd have kept it myself, but I love you."

Jessie said, "What is it?"

She took a small black crow out of the box. It had a yellow beak and gold eyes.

Jessie held it up and managed a little smile.

"Remember you told me on the phone about the crows here? Now you've got one of your own."

"The crows are what they call seniors here."

"Now you've got one of your own."

"There aren't any real crows here."

"Well, this is a crow, isn't it? . . . What do you mean the crows here aren't real crows?"

"I told you, Mother. That's what they call the seniors. They wear black capes."

"Oh, well, now you have a crow of your own. Do you see an ashtray anywhere around? I'm dying for a smoke."

"I don't think you'd better," Jessie said.

"I can't stay, anyway. We're opening in Baltimore tomorrow, in The Arena. . . . Oh, honey," she was kneeling beside Jessie now, "do you like it here?"

"So far . . . I can't take the crow back to Slaughter with me."

"Why do they call it Slaughter? What a gory name for a dorm!"

"It's named after a General Slaughter. . . . We aren't allowed to have stuffed animals."

Her mother brushed her hand through Jessie's hair. "I'll talk to General Reber about it."

Jessie said, "Don't. Keep the crow for me the way you keep Poison for me."

"I want you to have something, Jess. . . . Here, have this!" She reached behind her for the cuff watch. "Take this."

"That's too expensive, Mom."

"*Nothing* is too expensive for me to give to my little girl, honey. Here. I'll put it on you."

"It's way too big."

"No, it's flexible. See? *See?*"

She had the watch around Jessie's wrist.

She said, "It's yours, sweetheart! Skintight gave it to me! You know Skintight. He plays the sax with Filthy Lucre!"

Jessie just sat there.

Her mother took the crow from her hand and

held it up to her own face. "What is Mr. Crow's name, honey. Name him something."

"You name him. You keep him for me."

"I'll call him Mr. Crow."

Then Ike grabbed the crow from her hands and ran under the chair with it.

"Naughty, naughty dog!" Unique cried out.

Poison hissed.

That was the point when my father returned with my grandfather.

I ducked back inside my room.

When I finally come out of my room again, the house was quiet.

I went downstairs.

The long white limo was gone.

My father was walking Jessie back to Slaughter.

My grandfather had Ike out on a walk.

The crow was in pieces on the floor.

His sawdust insides were scattered everywhere.

CHAPTER NINE

Days later, while I walked my punishment tour in The Yard, I still obsessed about meeting Unique. Above her autograph in my notebook she wrote, "Go with the flow!" It was the name of one of her songs. In the video she made with Filthy Lucre, she danced with dead celebrities from Fred Astaire to John Kennedy, and then a masked man in a silver suit with a red scarf around his neck and a cowboy hat on, whisked her away riding a rocket.

"Go with the flow," she sang, *"You nev-ver, nev-er know."*

No one at BAM knew she was there.
My father said to keep it that way.
While I walked I thought of how Mom would get on the phone when anything important hap-

pened, and call my aunt Priscilla in New York City.

Whatever it was — a poem she finished, a raise my father got, her new little red Pontiac convertible — it was not real to her until she told her sister.

That was the way I felt about meeting Unique.

There was no one I could tell, not even Caleb. It was a flat and empty victory, like winning a foot race when no one you knew was watching or would ever hear of it.

On all the bulletin boards my father had posted a "request" for the cadet whose property *Thrasher* was to come forward and relieve the cadet walking punishment.

I walked and thought of Caleb, wrestling with his conscience, adding up the reports he already had listed against him so early in the semester, figuring there was no way he could step forward, even though my father knew it was his magazine.

We saw each other only in class, when there was no time for discussion. I finally passed him the note Jessie wanted me to give him and he opened it, hit his forehead with his fist, and said, "I don't *believe* her!"

Then he said, "She wants to be a Yard Bomber! *Why?*"

But that was all he had to say, and he could not look me in the eye.

We both knew *Thrasher* could be the final straw for Caleb, the ticket back to Maine. My father already had enough reports against Caleb to expel him. He was champing at the bit to get Caleb. Caleb was the one big weed in the perfect garden, the one off-key voice in the perfect chorus, the slight rattle in the well-tuned engine.

I walked my tour and thought of my conversation with Lieutenant Meadow, after I had turned in my English assignment.

She was an opera lover who resembled an opera singer in girth and tone of voice. We called her Heavy Meadow.

She said, "You get points for originality, Cadet Reber, but you didn't follow the assignment. I said I wanted a composition, not a cartoon strip."

"I couldn't think of anything to write." I had turned in the cartoon on impulse, hoping for some feedback. I doubted she'd ever tell The General anything about it. BAM faculty bent over backward to treat me like any other cadet.

"Besides," she said, "there is nothing really very funny about real lice, whether they live in books or not. . . . We had a head-lice epidemic just two years ago at Slaughter. Do you remember that?"

"These are just cartoon lice."

"Lice are lice. This Frankenlouse of yours doesn't have anything to do with family. Where's the family?"

"The other lice in the library were supposed to be — "

She cut me off.

"It's too far out. I said a *family*."

"You said it was up to us what kind of a family we wrote about."

"*Wrote* about. Not *drew*. This is not an art class, Cadet Reber."

"I wish we had one."

"We have one in art appreciation. And that's not the point, is it? I have to give you a failing grade because you did *not* follow the assignment." Then she trilled, "*Fol*-low the *assignment*, from now on!"

I walked my tour thinking about it . . . thinking that BAM ought to have a class for aspiring artists, something I'd mentioned before to The General.

He'd said there wasn't room in the curriculum, and there wasn't that much interest. I'd said there wasn't *any* interest in Famous Battles of

the Civil War, and that was in the curriculum.
. . . I'd gotten nowhere.

I walked and thought of my father in the living
room last night, the laptop computer on his
knees, frowning as he fumbled for the right
words while he composed his monthly Food For
Thought.

Reber males were not good writers. There was
a genetic reluctance to put down our thoughts.
There was something deep inside us that said *I
can't think of anything.*

My father issued one FFT the second Monday
of every month.

It was too many, my grandfather told him.
Even at Woo Poo we never got monthly guide-
lines. An FFT, he said, should come spontane-
ously, when something's happened to inspire it.

My father answered what he often answered:
Blister is *not* Woo Poo.

I walked and thought of my mother's latest
letter.

*When you come to visit me, I'll take you to the
Museum of American Illustration. Every famous il-
lustrator's work is there. Even cartoon strips are there.
You'll love it, Nick! . . . I am still looking for an*

apartment, staying with Priss until I find one. Every-
thing is very expensive, but I have found a job. It is
not high-paying but it is interesting. I work as a reader
at Jackson Publishing.

It was my second day of walking in The Yard,
an hour in the morning, an hour in the afternoon, an hour after retreat.

It had been raining all the while. I wore my
navy blue poncho and my light blue field cap. I
carried the mock M16 rifle.

Go with the flow.

I danced with Marilyn Monroe and waited for
the masked woman in the silver suit with the
red scarf and cowboy hat to arrive for liftoff on
the rocket.

CHAPTER
TEN

FOOD FOR THOUGHT

BLISTER is your home.

You are *always* welcome here!

If your parents' home is not available to you on *any* holiday, or in *any* season, BLISTER is.

All BLISTER asks of you is to respect its rules.

Respect yourself as a BLISTER cadet.

You will *never* have another home like this so honor it, use it, and do not abuse it!

You're at BLISTER, Mister!

CHAPTER ELEVEN

"Cadet Jessie Southgate relieving Cadet Nicolas Reber!"

"Cadet Nicolas Reber acknowledges!" (What are you *doing*, Jessie?)

"Cadet Jessie Southgate dismisses Cadet Nicolas Reber!" (I'm doing it for Caleb.)

(Why?)

(Because he can't do it! I've never been on Report so it won't hurt me to do it! *Move*, Nick!)

"Cadet Nicolas Reber acknowledges!" (Are you *sure* you want to do this?)

"Pre-sent arms!" (Yes, give me the gun!)

"Arms over!" (Thanks, Jessie. We owe you, Caleb and me!)

The house reeked of Glade air freshener.

Ike brought me half the head of Mr. Crow which he had gotten from his secret stash behind

the couch. Fanny knew about his stash and vac-
uumed around it. The last time I looked, there
was a Hartz rawhide chew stick half gone, an
old bedroom slipper of my mother's, his hard
blue ball, his hard red ball, his Squeaky Squirrel
minus the squeak, and his rubber hot dog.

I petted him and told him he'd soon suffer
from secondary smoke inhalation unless my
grandfather stopped hanging out with him.

"How did you get off Report?" my grandfather
said. He was reading *Sports Illustrated* in the armchair only my father sat in.

I told him about Jessie Southgate. I said I
thought she had a thing for Caleb.

"Speaking of Jessie Southgate, did you see
your father's September FFT? Blister is available
on *any* holiday and in *any* season?" Grandad had
gotten into the habit of having a mid-afternoon
Scotch. He took a sip. "I think he put that in
for Jessie. I think that mother of hers bothers
him."

"He put on full uniform for her."

"That was *before* he met her."

"Well, we're here all summer."

"We're not a boardinghouse. I told him: we're
going to be dumped on. All the ones that spend
the Christmas holidays with us are going to be
our summer guests."

"So we'll have Caleb and that crow whose family is in Egypt."

"*And* Jessie Southgate. You want to bet?"

Then he said, "Tell me about your cartoon strip."

"How do you know about it? From Heavy Meadow?"

"*Lieutenant* Meadow. She didn't tell anyone but me. . . . When do I see it?"

"It's just something I'm fooling with."

"I'd like to see it sometime."

"Is she going to tell Dad?"

"Of course not! Lieutenant Meadow wasn't tattling on you. I ran into her over in the library and she said you had a louse named Longfellow in this cartoon strip of yours. She remembered my recitation of a Longfellow poem at the Christmas party last year. She said this louse lives in that poem, and complains that a hungry and horrible creature from *Frankenstein* is eating him out of house and home."

HE EATS WHAT HE PLEASES!
H, I'S, AND E'ES,
A POET LIKE ME WHO IS GENTLE
CAN'T COPE WITH A LOUSE WHO IS MENTAL!

A MENTAL LOUSE IS IN THE HOUSE!

"She shouldn't have told you," I said.

" 'Hiawatha's Wooing' was your grandma's favorite poem . . . I'd like to see that cartoon strip."

"Maybe. Someday." That night I planned to draw the whole library with my little Mac mouse, to store in the computer.

"Whose idea is it to call the lieutenant 'Heavy Meadow'?"

"It's her nickname . . . like *you* call West Point 'Woo Poo.' "

"Woo Poo is affectionate. Heavy Meadow isn't. Was that Caleb's idea?"

"It's a takeoff on heavy *metal*. Why does Caleb always get the blame?"

He reached next to him and tossed me the new *TV Guide*. He said, "Look who's on the cover."

It was Caleb's father.

"Can I take this upstairs?"

"Oh, you're asking permission now."

I stuck it in my briefcase. "Don't tell Dad about the cartoon strip, okay?"

"I'm his father, Nick, not his stool pigeon. I don't know anything about cartoons, and you don't know anything about me having myself a Scotch in the afternoon."

I started upstairs. "Or about you sitting in his chair," I said.

He said, "Sitting in his chair and smoking."

"You better lay off the booze, Grandad. You're in a good mood and it shows."

He recited the Longfellow poem as I went up the staircase . . . *From the waterfall he named her, Minnehaha, Laughing Water.*

But Frankenlouse had been busy. Now the line read   *om   a rf ll   nam   r, M nn a a   aug   ng Wat r.*

Not just Longfellow, but all the book lice feared Frankenlouse. Soon the one big event of the year would take place: The Great Louse Hop. But no one believed that it would be a happy time with a monster loose in their library.

CHAPTER
TWELVE

Last year when I hung out at Fort Slaughter,
Caleb would show me his "mail" from his famous father.

Peter Purr never wrote. He sent cassettes
which Caleb played on the VCR in the living
room there.

Usually his father was sitting at his desk
in his office at General Broadcasting Company.
Behind him were the tall buildings at Rocke-
feller Center. He favored blazers with gold buttons, and he always wore an ascot around his
neck.

"Hello, Son," he began his video letters.
"How are you?"

Once Caleb stopped the tape abruptly.

He turned to me wide-eyed and said, "Nick!
Did you *hear* that?"

"Did I hear what?"

"Did you *hear* what my father just said?"

"What?"

"I can't believe it!"

"What?"

"He wants to know how I am!"

Then Caleb rolled himself into a ball on the rug and began laughing.

On the cover of *TV Guide* he was pictured under an umbrella with a wide grin of white caps in an even row. He looked about thirty. The headline read: PETER PURR PURRS.

Under that, "I have other plans, other goals."

And under that, "America's favorite weatherman speaks out on his ambitions, and why he calls Maine home."

There were photographs of Purrfield, Caleb's home on a cliff overlooking the ocean.

Caleb's young stepmother was holding two babies in her arms.

I skimmed the article. There was no mention of Caleb's mother, who'd died of breast cancer.

The last paragraph said:

At this point, Juliet Purr swept into the room with the couple's pride and joy, the year-old Purr twins,

Snow and Rain, followed by a very cross-eyed cat called Slush, who galloped over to claw a side of the elegant George I armchair. . . . No wonder he calls Maine home!

There was no mention of Caleb.

CHAPTER THIRTEEN

My father liked to say my mother "toyed" with the arts. She was interested in everything to do with art, theater, and music, that was true, but her great love was ballet. She'd started dancing when she was nine, and she had danced at the Old Dominion Center right up until she left for New York.

That was how she came to appear in the Old Dominion Players' production of *The Nutcracker*.

It was a Christmas show three years before she went, the same year Aaron Bindle arrived at BAM.

He was the only cadet who performed in the show. The children were recruited from the Old Dominion elementary and middle schools. Townspeople played other roles.

My father and I sat in the audience with a

contingent from BAM. A lot of the guys were restless through the first act because it was ballet, and no one they knew was on stage.

Then came the second act: my mother dancing the role of the Sugarplum Fairy, in her white tights and pink tutu, gliding through the Kingdom of Sweets.

The guys roared their approval, clapped, and whistled, for if my father was not a favorite with them, she was.

My father winced and shifted his weight in the folding chair.

Finally, Aaron Bindle made his grand entrance, with what looked like a whole bunch of bananas stuffed down the front of his tights.

Aaron didn't really need to talk. Aaron had attitude going for him. The only thing most people knew about Aaron, besides his interest in ballet, was his refusal to dissect frogs in science lab . . . and his anger at the collection of live frogs and white mice the lab kept for experiments. Aaron seldom wrote down anything, preferring to communicate with his eyes and eyebrows and the hard or soft lines he could make with his mouth. He was known for his pantomime quarrels with Captain Stuart, the science teacher, all centering around the animals kept in cages in the lab. But there were also daily

messages scrawled across the blackboard in the
lab: things like No SKIN OFF YOUR BACK, CAP-
TAIN STUART! . . . and STOP CRUELTY TO SMALL
CREATURES!

The night of *The Nutcracker*, Aaron's attitude
was shining like a full sun at noon in a hot
summer sky. Aaron was elegant and lofty that
night. Six foot something, he was thin and mus-
cular, with those dark eyes, eyebrows, and thick
black hair, and the high cheekbones, the perfect
nose, the wide lips, and great white teeth.

The BAM cadets clapped as hard for him as
they would have for a rock star, a basketball star,
or the highest paid player in the NFL.

Later my father believed that some of them
knew what was happening back at the science
lab . . . that the applause was as much for that,
as for the way Aaron danced.

When the dance listed as the *grand pas de deux*
began, with Aaron, the Cavalier; and Mom, the
Sugarplum Fairy, my father's face became the
color of the red flint spearhead on one of his
medals.

He was already furious.

We didn't show affection easily in our family,
except for my mother. We kissed at airports
when one of us was leaving or arriving, and at
holidays and birthdays. My father could not

even say ordinary words of endearment like "honey" or "sweetheart," and my mother would sometimes tease him about it . . . and sometimes take me aside and tell me not to be afraid of those words. "Lighten up, Nick: Those words won't hurt you. Hugs and kisses won't, either."

Aaron was so confident and graceful as he danced with my mother, you forgot he was only fourteen. And Mom looked like a kid, no where near thirty-six.

It was not a suggestive dance, not anything like the kind Unique did on MTV, but my father's face was the kind of thundercloud it would have been if it had been like that.

He was saved from exploding by an Old Dominion Players member who sneaked down the aisle, crouched by my father, and whispered something which made my father take off abruptly.

He wasn't there for the curtain calls. My mother and Aaron got the most applause: Mom with her face radiant and smiling; Aaron, his usual aloof self, only one flash of the perfect teeth, then his eyes staring straight ahead, one wet lock of his thick, black hair falling across his forehead.

Mom and I had to wait for a taxi to take us

home, since my father had rushed back to Blister in his white Jeep.

There had been a fire in the science lab, a small building separate from the main barracks.

The lab was destroyed.

My father arrived back at our house just as we did. He assured us no one was hurt, the fire was out.

Mom removed the red rose corsage pinned to her coat.

"Thanks for the flowers, Patch. We usually get these on closing night."

"They're not from me, they're from your sister," said my father, "but this *is* closing night."

"What does that mean, Patch?"

"It means you'll have the decency to let your understudy take over the role."

"But why? We don't have understudies!"

"Someone will take over your role!"

"Why? And who?"

"It was a humiliation for me, that's why. Do you have any idea how I felt seeing you dance with that boy in those tight pants he *stuffed*?"

"All male dancers wear codpieces, Patch!"

"Not when they dance with *my* wife!"

That was the point when I was sent upstairs to my room.

He did not know that night anything about

the fact that the animals were not in the fire. A janitor reported the next morning that the empty cages where the mice and frogs were kept had been found in the basement of Eisenhower, the BAM drama barracks.

At first, it was speculated that firemen had rescued the animals, and put them in the basement, since it was next door to the lab.

But by mid-afternoon there was talk that Aaron had been seen near the lab, shortly before he left for the performance of *The Nutcracker*.

Aaron insisted that he was not involved in the fire-setting, and no one could prove otherwise.

The firemen determined that the blaze had begun in a wastebasket where a cigarette had been dropped.

Captain Stuart was a smoker, and so were a few of the maintenance men.

No one ever knew the truth.

No one ever saw a second performance of *The Nutcracker*, either.

My father had his way.

That *had* been closing night. Since my mother was right about there being no understudies, the show had to be cancelled. There was no way my father was going to back down, and when it

came to anything he felt would hurt Blister, she
always gave in to him.

It was anyone's guess what had really happened, but I think my mother believed that
Aaron was not connected to the fire . . . that the
fire had just become my father's excuse for pre-
venting her from dancing ever again with Aaron.

The incident was never brought up in our
house after that. But I think way back then was
when she made up her mind she was leaving
him.

CHAPTER FOURTEEN

Halloween morning I leaned down, took a spoonful of Rice Krispies, and my father said, "That's a dollar you owe the kitty, Nick."

"I didn't duck."

"You ducked, Nick. Put a dollar in the kitty before you leave."

"I think I'll start taking my meals at Mess like everyone else."

"Be my guest. But if you take meals there, you take all your meals there."

"Yum-yum," said my grandfather. "Spanish rice Mondays, baked beans Tuesdays, chili chow Wednesdays — "

My father interrupted. "What kind of costume are you getting together for tonight?"

"I'm going as Frankenstein's monster."

My grandfather announced, "My entrance at the party, *ce soir*, will be a surprise."

My father said, "I hope *you're* not wearing a *costume?*"

"I said my *entrance*, not my costume."

"Because I don't think you should wear a costume," my father said.

"I don't intend to wear a costume."

"You could come in uniform as I do. You have your uniform. That would be perfectly proper."

"Don't tell me what to wear or what is proper!"

"You do have your uniform?"

"I am retired now, and so is my uniform!"

"There's no need to shout, Father!"

He turned back to me. "And did you ask Jessie Southgate to go with you, as I suggested?"

"I asked her, sir, but she has a date."

"Not with Caleb!"

"No, sir." Jessie made Caleb uncomfortable. Caleb kept asking me what she wanted? . . . *You*, I'd tell him. He'd make the kind of face my grandfather would when he was served okra. Caleb hadn't made the transition from skateboards to girls.

My father said, "I have no use for Caleb . . . ever since he talked that child into taking the blame for what he did."

"You had no use for Caleb long before that, sir," I said. There was no use in trying to tell him it was Jessie's own idea to take the blame.

"Who is Jessie going with then?"

"Aaron," I said.

"Aaron *Bindle*?"

"He's the only Aaron at BAM, sir."

I saw an imaginary balloon over his head with the Cavalier inside dancing in the Kingdom of Sweets with the Sugarplum Fairy.

"How old is Aaron Bindle?"

"Seventeen, sir."

"I didn't know an upperclassman would date a worm," said my father.

"Probably he wouldn't before this year, sir," I said, "since that would have made him gay." It was our first year with females enrolled.

"We don't say gay," my father said. "Gay means elated. We say homosexual."

"*They* say, gay, sir."

"We don't. We say homosexual," said my father. "I don't like the idea of a seventeen-year-old with a twelve-year-old."

"You wanted females here," said my grandfather, who didn't.

"I think they're just friends from dance class, sir," I said. "They don't really *date*."

"You keep an eye on Jessie, Nick. Will you do that?"

"Yes, sir."

I was going to the party in tandem with a new buddy.

He was a junior at Blister. Kinya Powell, a black guy from New York City. He had two other friends who were black but they were crows.

Crows hung out mostly with crows.

Kinya was going to the Halloween party as Frankenstein.

Before I left for classes I got my copy of *Frankenstein* from my room. Kinya wanted to glance at it before that evening.

I hadn't opened it since my mother gave it to me.

For the first time I saw the inscription inside.

For Terri, Because you like horror stories and because my love for you is monstrous! P.

I had to read it twice to believe my father wrote it.

On my way out, I stopped in the hall to put the dollar I owed for ducking for my food into the blue vase, which was our kitty.

At the end of the year, the money was donated to the Old Dominion Hospital.

Before *The Nutcracker* three years ago, it used to go to the Old Dominion Players.

CHAPTER FIFTEEN

At BAM, Halloween was major!

It was the one time cadets could dress as they pleased.

The crows were the only ones who dressed alike, and their entrance from The Yard was a dynamite beginning to the evening in the gym.

They wore luminescent skeleton suits, with their black capes over their shoulders, black gloves, and silver masks across their eyes. They came silently, in single file from The Yard, marching slowly with their legs extended between steps . . . ten steps . . . stop . . . all look to the right . . . ten steps . . . stop . . . all look to the left, until they reached the door.

As they marched inside they sang "The Crows Farewell," the last song sung at every Blister graduation.

Now into your midst Crows come,
Ta-rum!
We made good friends and studied some,
Ta-rum!
Farewell, good-bye, and so it goes,
Ta-rum!
And where it ends, God only knows!
Ta-rum! Ta-rum!

That song always sounded eerie, but more so with the crows dressed up as skeletons.

Since BAM had admitted females, some cadets made dates with them, and some invited town girls for the occasion. But Halloween night was traditionally a game night, where cadets vied for prizes of movie passes, CDs, books, and slips excusing them from morning formation, allowing cadets who won these slips to sleep in and even skip breakfast.

On the right, inside the door, Jessie Southgate waited with the other females who were crows' dates.

She had managed to put together a skateboarder's costume. She had cutoff pants, a Yard Bombers' shirt, tube socks, Doc Martens, and a yellow leather Kangol cap worn backward.

I watched Aaron leave the crows' formation and go over to her. He stood beside her like a scarecrow keeping the birds away. . . . When Aaron was out of his room, where the machine was which could talk for him, he never wrote notes, never signed, though he knew sign language. Aaron was just there. He always looked straight ahead. Jessie would glance up at him occasionally — it was a long way up, she was so little — but he kept his eyes on the room, like some FBI agent guarding a member of the president's family.

The moment Caleb appeared in the gym, I knew the hours I spent making myself into Frankenstein's monster were a total waste.

Caleb looked as though he was caked with blood. An eye was hanging down his face. Half an ear was off, and he seemed to be holding in guts which spilled out of his stomach. His clothes were rags. He looked as though he had been caught in an explosion. Bloody bandages were attached to his neck, ankle, wrist, and forehead. He had on only one shoe. The other bare foot seemed to be missing toes.

The sign on Caleb read COLLATERAL DAMAGE.

It was military talk for destruction caused by something like a megaton bomb which landed on "nonactive personnel," — army language for civilians.

Kinya looked at him and said, "Excellent!"

From way across the gym I could feel the drumbeat of my father's heart as he eyed Caleb. His mouth was twitching as it did when he was making an effort to keep the anger that was mushrooming inside his guts from curling out of his mouth.

Kinya had put minimal effort into his costume. A black civie suit with a white shirt and black necktie. He'd found a top hat at Eisenhower, where most of the cadets had gone for their costumes.

His name tag said VICTOR FRANKENSTEIN.

Mine said, FRANKENSTEIN'S MONSTER.

If Caleb hadn't shown up, I might have passed for one. I'd tried. I'd made my skin yellow, my lips black, combed my straight black hair forward in bangs, put a screw in my neck, and put on a black sacklike suit — actually a pair of old black silk pajamas of my father's.

The faculty dressed up, too, except for Colonel Flagg, second in command, in the Blister uniform as my father was.

Captain Tuttle was a ghoul, which didn't take much makeup, and there were other officers disguised as vampires, Godzilla, Dracula, and Jekyll/Hydes.

The BAM orchestra played "The March of The Wooden Soldiers" as the littlest worms arrived from Slaughter, the seven, eight, and nine-year-olds. There were a lot of Mutant Ninja Turtles, a Kermit the Frog, some Dr. Seuss characters, and two Terminators.

Kinya and I saw each other as soul buddies since we both had ambitions to be something: me, a cartoonist and Kinya, a geophysicist.

While I walked around thinking of my book lice, inventing words for the balloons over their heads, Kinya wondered about things like how much dry land would be lost if the polar ice caps were to melt completely, causing the sea level to rise.

I think it pissed Caleb off that we had this in common, or maybe Caleb just didn't like my having a new buddy.

Caleb would tell me that Kinya was as boring as a glacier was cold, and who *cared* about the Antarctic ice sheet, anyway?

Caleb never wondered who cared about skateboarding. He was as linear in his conversation as my father was in his thinking. Straight ahead. Straight ahead.

He talked about the big contest coming up between the BAM Yard Bombers and Augusta Military Academy's Plank Pilots — long enough for Kinya to start looking up at the ceiling which was fastened with balloons. And Kinya yawned,

too. Caleb saw the yawn, kept talking anyway:
about up curbies and 360 kick flips, backside tail
slides, and switch-foot heel flips.

I tried to change the subject.

"Where'd Jessie get that shirt?"

"From me. It's on loan, like this is," Caleb
said.

He pulled up his sleeve and showed me the
gold cuff watch.

He said, "Neat, huh?"

"She's letting you wear that thing?"

"It was her deal. She only gets my shirt
and cap for tonight. I get to wear this for a
week."

I could see Jessie down the room bobbing for
apples, trying for a slip to miss morning formation. Aaron stood close by, all the more mysterious in his silver mask.

Kinya had drifted over to a dart game.

I told Caleb, "You better not lose that watch."

"She wouldn't care if I did. She's like glue,
Nick. I can't get her off me at Slaughter."

"You shouldn't have made the deal. She was
looking for an in."

"I like this watch. Skintight gave it to her
mother. It says — "

"I know what it says."

"It says: 'Watch where you go without me.' I like that. And Skintight is the only rock star I like. He used to be a skateboarder. He was professional until he was eighteen." Then Caleb nudged my appendix with his elbow, and grinned. "Hey, did you see your old man look at me?"

"I saw him."

I could see him looking at me, too.

At me, then back at Jessie and Aaron.

I wandered over their way, remembering my promise to keep an eye on Jessie.

Aaron had a white handkerchief out and he was wiping off her chin.

She said, "We're going to get in line for The Grand March. I bet Caleb will win best costume."

Aaron put his handkerchief back and crooked his arm for her to take.

She said, "Ask Caleb to show you the watch he's wearing."

"I saw it."

"That's my watch, Nick!" On my little Mac computer you have your choice of predrawn features: surprise, anger, joy, sadness. But nothing there could catch the combination of uncertainty and pleasure that was on Jessie's face, as though

she believed something she maybe shouldn't
. . . and that was right: She believed she was
getting somewhere with Caleb, and *shouldn't* —
forget *maybe*.

I didn't have a clue as to what there was about
Caleb that got to Jessie. Life's mysteries, my
mother used to say, are really never fathomable:
We just make up answers because we're not
supposed to let on we don't have any.

Aaron nudged her until she put her hand up
on his arm. He gave me a look. It said to get
lost.

I never thought my mother was right about
Aaron not having anything to do with the fire
in the science lab. Much as I didn't like to agree
with my father, I did on that point. I knew things
about Aaron none of the other cadets did, because of my post by the banister upstairs in our
house.

France Bindle had committed suicide.

When Aaron applied for admission, my father
learned all he could about Aaron. He had long
felt it was past time to admit more disabled ap-
plicants. But in Aaron's case he wanted to make
sure his mind wasn't messed up . . . that his
being mute didn't have to do with his father's
taking his own life. He discovered that Aaron
had become mute way before that, for a reason

no doctors could figure out. In every other way he was supposed to be normal, and probably better than normal academically.

Maybe his father's suicide had something to do with Aaron's role as The Great Protector. Maybe being mute since he was seven years old had done it. Or maybe both.

For whatever reason, Aaron was a watcher over the weak and helpless . . . not exactly the way you'd think the daughter of Unique might be described . . . unless you met her.

Jessie had this thing about her: You wanted to look out for her (even my father did . . . particularly my father).

Caleb might have felt the same way, except I think she scared Caleb. A guy without a chin who still put Oxy on his pimples every night, and wasn't wanted home, had a hard time with the idea someone was drooling over him.

Over her shoulder Jessie said to me, "Don't you think Caleb's got the best costume?"

Aaron was actually pulling her with him.

I said, yeah, Caleb had the best costume.

There was a drumroll from the BAM orchestra.

Everyone started racing to line up for The Grand March.

But Jessie stopped in her tracks and stared down toward the doorway.

"Whoa!" she exclaimed, and she pressed a hand to her mouth.

Aaron was staring in the same direction.

What came through the door would stop us all: Heavy Meadow, out of uniform, lumbering forward in a long black dress that came to her ankles, high heels, her brown hair out of its bun and flowing down her back, some kind of yellow flower pinned above her voluminous bosom.

Behind her, a Peter Purr-type blue blazer with gold buttons, and gray flannel pants. Black hair with silver strands that shined and glistened in the overhead track lighting.

"Who's the old dude struggling to keep up with her?" Jessie asked.

And because Aaron couldn't answer, I did.

"My grandfather," I said. "That's my grandfather."

"Whoa! Ex-cussssse me, Nick!"

I looked for my father. He was easy to see. He was the one with the color rising from the neck of his uniform up to his face. The one with the eyes popping out and the jaw tightening.

The BAM orchestra was beginning "O Blister, My Blister!"

Balloons dropped from the ceiling.

CHAPTER SIXTEEN

Dearest Nicky,

Daddy said it's okay for you to come for Thanksgiving. I know you hate wearing your uniform outside Old Dominion, so just come in old clothes, but bring a sport coat in case we have dinner out and go to theater.

Daddy said a cadet named Kinta(?) is coming to New York that weekend, too, so ask him if he wants a ride in from the airport, since Priscilla and I will drive out to meet your plane.

Nicky, dear, don't do anything to get Daddy mad because I don't want him to have a reason to change his mind.

Give Ike a big hug for me and tell Grandad I miss him.

Love, Mom

P.S. I thought of you last night. We saw a play based on The Hobbit, *with Gollum in it. Remember when you used to pretend you were Gollum? Remember when you would hide under the bed and say, "Sssshe'sss looking for usss, Preciousss, isss sssshe?"*

CHAPTER SEVENTEEN

Lieutenant Meadow held forth at the black-board.

She was writing down the names of weirdos from Charles Dickens's novel *Hard Times*.

Mrs. Sparsit.

James Harthouse.

Tom Gradgrind.

Josiah Bounderby.

"Listen to those names! Dickens had great names for his characters!"

Someone yelled, "Slackbridge!"

"Yes," Heavy Meadow looked ecstatic, "Slackbridge!"

Outside the wind was blowing the last of the fall leaves from the trees.

The Little Soldiers were marching from their classes to lunch at Slaughter.

Under the American flag on the flagpole was

the black crow flag, light blue with a black crow stitched on it. It was at half-mast because a crow was being court-martialed for smoking. At that very moment the cadet sat in senior barracks waiting for an underclassman of his choice to take his *Mea Culpa*. Crows never took another crow's confession of wrongdoing. I knew the court-martial was a mere technicality. My father was expelling Foster Todd. He was black, a friend of Kinya's. By day's end he would be on a plane to New York. The ticket was already on my father's desk in our living room.

Heavy Meadow was the subject of much conversation in our house. My father wasn't happy about his father dating a BAM officer, much less one my father's age.

Evenings, my father had to take Ike for his walk. Then he would sit in the armchair with his eyeshade on, his wristwatch beside him on the table, waiting for my grandfather to come home.

My father'd ask him where they'd gone and then go ballistic and shout, "*Why* do you sit in that public barroom for all of Old Dominion to see you carrying on like an old fool with one of our young officers?"

My grandfather would answer that most bar-rooms *were* public, and anyway it was not a bar-room, it was the Old Dominion Hotel, and she was never in uniform.

Ike sat out these tirades under the dining room table. I could just leave my bedroom door open and catch most of the action.

"Where do you suppose Dickens got his ideas for such characters?" Heavy Meadow asked.

Caleb raised his hand. (The cuff watch was still on his wrist, though it had been weeks since the deal with Jessie.)

Caleb said, "Dickens's father went to prison and the family was so poor that Dickens had to go to work as a drudge."

Caleb had read his Cliff Notes, too. I recognized the wording, the "drudge." I tuned out.

I would rather talk about where Walt Kelly got his idea for "Pogo," where Charles Schulz got his for "Peanuts," or where Garry Trudeau's "Doonesbury" came from.

I had my Frankenlouse sketchbook with me. Jessie was the inspiration for my new female louse, Sugarplum. She lived in *The Nutcracker* libretto. Frankenlouse wanted to ask her to The Great Louse Hop, the big event everyone now feared would turn into The Great Louse Flop, with a monster loose. But Frankenlouse had a big flaw, for a monster louse. He could not look at, eat, or even say the letter *m* (the one letter monster lice were known to crave!). He would have to call her "Sugarplu," and he feared ridicule almost as much as the letter *m* repelled him.

I was stopped at that point. Blocked again!

I was also thinking about poor Foster Todd, sitting in Patton Barracks, still holding out hope, and waiting for the humiliating ordeal of telling an underclassman he'd smoked a Camel on Halloween night out behind the gym.

"Cadet Reber? Ca-*det Reber*!"

"Yes, Lieutenant!"

"Come down from outer space and tell the class something *you* remember from *Hard Times*."

"I remember Mr. Sleary . . . the way he talked."

"What about it? How did he talk?"

"He said things like 'People mutht be amuthed. They can't be alwayth a-learning, not yet they can't be alwayth a-working, they ain't made for it.' "

"Why do you suppose you remember that?"

"Because his way of talking is so different."

She called on someone else next, but a light had gone on in my head. Once a writer named Paul Zindel had come to BAM to talk about his books. While he was telling us in this quiet voice that sometimes an idea came suddenly, there was a BANG like a gunshot, surprising everyone. He'd set off a firecracker to demonstrate his point.

I could hear my own BANG that morning.

After my mother had written the P.S. about Gollum in her letter, I had added *The Hobbit* to my louse library. Gollum used to be my favorite character in that book.

He was a small, slimy, web-footed creature with pale eyes sticking out, who talked only to himself. He hissed his words. He called himself "My precioussss."

I had planned to have him mentioned as Sugarplum's love but not to have him say anything.

But now I wondered what if Gollum is wise to Frankenlouse's secret; what if he comes forth to tell on him?

WHY DOES HE NEVER SSSAY OR EAT A WORD WITH "M" IN IT? ISSS NOT THE LETTER "M" THE SSSINGULAR MONSSSTER DELICACY?

YES! "M" IS!
"M" IS!

After class, Caleb waited for me.

"My old man is coming to town tomorrow night to take me to dinner."

"Good!"

"So he won't have the guilts about not inviting me to Purrfield for Thanksgiving."

"I'm going to New York."

"I'm going to New York. I'm going to New York. I'm going to New York. I've turned into a parrot."

"Sorry. I forgot I told you."

"Kinya's going, too. Kinya's going, too. Kinya's going, too."

"Okay, okay! I forgot I mentioned it."

"You want to have dinner with me and the weatherman?"

"Sure!"

"It'll relieve him. He never knows what to say to me when we're alone . . . not that we've ever been alone since I was four."

"I'll sign up for OPEL." We got one Off-Premise Evening Leave a month, in the company of an adult.

"At last we'll get a steak out of it," said Caleb.

I forgot to ask him how come he still had the cuff watch.

CHAPTER
EIGHTEEN

I wasn't due at the Old Dominion Hotel until seven, but my father told me to finish dressing by six-thirty. He had something to say to me before I left.

The Anti-Bias Equality League was on his neck because of Foster Todd's expulsion. Besides fending off phone calls from ABEL headquarters, he was busy getting *The Richmond Times* out of the library. Unique was in the headlines again: something about drugs found in her car when she was arrested for speeding in Pennsylvania. There was a photograph of her handcuffed, on her way to police headquarters.

I wore the dress uniform required for OPELs. The light blue jacket, the white garrison belt, the dark blue pants with the red stripes down the sides.

My father was eating dinner alone in the dining room.

When I ate alone in that room, at that long table, I read something, or listened to my Walkman. But he just sat there eating, and frowning down at his food. He was never in a good mood, anyway, when someone was expelled, but ABEL wouldn't get off his back. He was suppose to list any white cadets who'd been expelled in the last three years (but no one had been tossed out for five years). It'd been over seven years since a crow had gotten the boot.

He looked up at me as I walked into the dining room and he said, "Do you call that belt clean?"

"It's not very dirty, sir."

"Not very dirty is not clean. Change it before you leave."

"Yes, sir."

"After you change it, you're to go to Slaughter to pick up Cadet Southgate. She is joining you for dinner."

"Caleb didn't say anything about that, sir."

"Maybe Collateral Damage wanted to surprise you."

He touched his napkin to his lips to hide the small smile there. He had been calling Caleb "Collateral Damage," privately, ever since Halloween. It was a joke and it wasn't. My father's witticisms often masked displeasure, such as when he called my aunt Priscilla "Aunt Prissilly." He blamed my mother's decision to leave him on my aunt. He believed my mother'd met this phantom man on one of her visits to my aunt's in New York.

I said, "I thought Unique had to give permission if Jessie took an OPEL?" I was trying to think how she could do that from jail.

My father said, *"Mrs. Southgate* gave her permission. Apparently, Caleb got his father to set this up some time ago. I think *you* were a last minute decision on Caleb's part."

"Why isn't Caleb picking her up?"

"Because he's already at the hotel with his father. . . . And, Nick?"

"Yes, sir?"

"Say nothing about Mrs. Southgate's arrest in Pennsylvania."

"You don't have to tell me that, sir."

"I know that, but I'm telling you just the same."

"Yes, sir."

I felt badly leaving him there eating roast beef by himself, the answering machine blaring out messages from ABEL, Foster Todd's father, and the local black minister from the Old Dominion Baptist Church.

Ike was waiting right around the corner from the dining room, just in case my father broke down and shared some of his roast beef with him. Ike kept inching forward, shaking his head so the dog tags on his collar would rattle and remind my father he was there, and he liked roast beef, too.

"Where's Grandad, sir?"

"How do *I* know?"

"Yes, sir."

"Ike!" my father roared. "Get back in the living room!"

Ike's head disappeared from view.

"Well, I'll be going, sir."

"Just go!"

"Have a good evening, sir."

He grumbled something back that had the words "you, too," in it, and ducked for his roast beef . . . I didn't point it out. Thanksgiving was too close to push my luck.

The Little Soldiers wore dark tops and light bottoms, the reverse of ours. BAM hadn't yet issued skirts for females; it was still under debate.

But Jessie had her hair undone, a small infraction of the rules, and it spilled to her shoulders as we walked down Blister Hill in the cold autumn evening.

"Does your mother know Peter Purr?" I asked her.

"Only from television. I couldn't believe it when her secretary called me last week and told me I was invited tonight. Caleb's so weird, Nick. He didn't even mention it to me. But he must have written his father about me weeks ago, because it was all arranged through their secretaries."

"I thought maybe you had another deal. He could wear your watch and you'd get to meet his father. I saw the watch on his wrist yesterday."

"I don't care about his father. I care about Caleb!"

"I know that."

"I really, really care about him. I wouldn't be amazed if I loved him and I wouldn't be amazed if he loved me, too."

I was beginning to think romance was a very sneaky business. One day when you weren't looking, something happened to change someone you thought you knew until you suddenly saw them with another person, and they were different . . . my grandfather and Heavy Meadow . . . and now Caleb.

"He can't admit he loves me, Nick. He didn't even say, 'See you tonight' when I saw him at Slaughter today."

I couldn't figure out why Caleb had dragged me into it. Maybe Jessie was right. Maybe Caleb couldn't face the evening without someone along to defuse it, so it wouldn't seem as though she was a date — we were just friends of Caleb invited to dinner with his father. A smoke screen of some kind.

"He loves wearing my watch, Nick, but he can't even admit that. He just wears it, and I don't say anything. I'm getting like him: I just don't say anything."

I didn't have anything to say, either.

"I think he won't let me in The Yard Bombers because I make him too nervous."

"What does he say?"

"I'm telling you: We hardly talk. It's weird, Nick! It's the most weird, exciting thing that's ever happened to me. . . . I'm glad, too, because Aaron's machine tells me that Caleb has a skateboarder's mentality, that skateboarders don't have any sex appeal."

"Not like machines do."

She giggled. "Well, that machine of Aaron's has its charms, Nick. I swear I forget it's Aaron's mind at work. It's like it's got a personality all its own. More personality than Caleb has, not that I care. I love that boy just the way he is.''

I was hoping she'd drop the subject of Caleb.

She asked, ''Have you heard Aaron's machine?''

''Once,'' I said. ''It calls me Ick.''

''It can say Nick. It can say anything. He's just programmed it to say Ick.''

''What's he got against *me*?''

''He thinks you and your father were mean to your mother. I think he had a thing for your mother . . . Nick?''

''What?''

''Do I look pretty? I hate wearing pants all the time.''

''You look pretty,'' I said. She did, too. If she'd heard anything about her mother being in jail, it didn't show. She was bouncing along beside me on a high. I couldn't believe Caleb Purr was the cause of it. I was glad BAM had admitted females because I had a lot to learn about them.

CHAPTER NINETEEN

Peter Purr was purring at us.

Well, not at *us*. Not at Caleb and me. He was purring at Jessie.

He was probably the only man in Old Dominion, maybe in the whole state of Virginia, with a silk ascot around his neck, and a tan on his face — I *think* it was a tan.

He had on one of his famous blazers with brass buttons and another square of silk hanging out of his breast pocket. His Gucci loafers were polished and tasseled. His nails were manicured. He smelled of cologne. He smiled at Jessie, and at his own reflection in the mirror behind her, and he talked so loud everyone in the room was watching our table.

He'd ordered steaks "all the way around," and a small half-bottle of wine for himself, which he sent back for a replacement because there was cork floating in it.

He'd produced the latest copy of *Thrasher* to keep Caleb busy between bites of porterhouse, and from time to time he'd include me by saying, "Everything okay, Rick?"

I'd corrected him a few times, then I'd gotten used to the "Rick." It was different, anyway. I was always being called Nick. It was a change.

I'd tune out and tune in again, and whenever I tuned in again, he was on the same subject.

He'd heard Unique was up for a lead role in a sitcom about talk radio. She was going to be cast as part of a team of right-wing commentators on a call-in show.

The more Jessie said she didn't know anything about it, the more Peter Purr told her about it, and about himself.

"I never wanted to be a weatherman. What did I know about weather when I first blew in from Maine? But they had this opening at GBS, and they liked my delivery. Weather is all delivery, you know, Jessie."

Caleb would show me these photographs of guys on skateboards in midair, and he'd tell me this one was doing an "upcurbie" and that one was doing an "ollie."

Jessie kept looking across the table at him, but

he couldn't seem to focus in her direction.

"Now I've always hated Hollywood," Peter Purr continued, "and I hear this show is being shot right in New York."

"My mother hates Hollywood, too."

"Your mother's right! Hollywood isn't for real actors — it's for the losers who can't make it in New York! Your mother can make it anywhere! Unique is the kind of great star I'd be *honored* to work with!"

At this point, Caleb snored and let his head drop to one side.

"Are we keeping you up, mister?" his father said.

"I could use an extra blanket," Caleb said.

"Very funny, Caleb."

"Thanks, Dad."

"Caleb's a world-class comedian, Jessie," Peter Purr said, "We should all stop our conversation and let him crack some jokes."

"You're the only one having a conversation," said Caleb. "We all are just listening."

"Let's hear a joke, son. We're all ears."

"This whole evening's a joke," said Caleb.

"I'm having a good time, Caleb," Jessie said, as though she thought Caleb was complaining on her account.

Peter Purr clamped a big hand down on her

wrist and said, "We can go right on with our good time, Jessie. . . . You're having a good time, aren't you, Rick?"

"Yes, sir," I said. What was I supposed to say?

Caleb said, "Rick's never had a better time. He's got a new name and everything."

"What's that supposed to mean, wise guy?" Peter Purr said.

"That's supposed to mean Rick's name is Nick."

"Why didn't you say so, Nick?"

"I got to like the name Rick," I said.

Jessie giggled.

"It's very gratifying to make the effort to come all the way to Virginia to find my son in such a sulky mood, wouldn't you say, Jessie?"

"Caleb's mood is all right with me," said Jessie.

"Because you're a lady, Jessie. You go with the flow — as your mother likes to sing." Then Peter Purr actually sang. "Go with the flow. You nev-er nev-er know."

Caleb clapped. "Encore!" he said in a bored tone. "Bravo! If you don't get in the new sitcom, you could try a singing career."

Peter Purr smiled across the table at him. "You just lost three months allowance, big shot!"

"He was just teasing," Jessie said.

"He was just being rude, Jessie."

That was the point when I heard a familiar voice make a familiar complaint.

". . . hate okra!" echoed through the dining room.

"Oh migosh!" Jessie said. "Your grandfather's here with Heavy Meadow!"

They were back in the smoking section.

On my way out of the dining room, I stopped at their table.

My grandfather said, "We could hear that pompous ass all the way back here!"

"We heard you, too, Grandad."

"Your grandfather hates okra," Lieutenant Meadow said. "And I agree. Its oozy tasting."

They were holding hands under the table while they had their coffee and Grandfather smoked a cigarette with his other hand. Heavy Meadow was all dressed up in a bright green dress with pearls around her neck and pearl earrings.

Grandfather said, "I want to see this Frankenstein cartoon strip, Nick! Why are you holding out on me?"

"I bet I know why," Heavy Meadow said. "He's afraid you'll tell you-know-who."

"The strip's called Franken*louse*."

"Speaking of you-know-who," she said.

"It's not really him," I said. "It might have started off being him, but it's changed."

Up front by the door, Peter Purr was giving autographs. Jessie was standing there staring at Caleb, who was standing there staring at *Thrasher*.

My grandfather said, "Tell you-know-who not to wait up for me, Nick!"

CHAPTER
TWENTY

You believe what you want to believe. Jessie
didn't want to believe that Peter Purr had
planned the whole evening to angle his way into
Unique's sitcom.

In the cab, on the way back to Blister, Jessie
kept thanking Caleb for inviting her along. And
Caleb was nice enough not to tell her he had
nothing to do with it.

"You'd better give me *Thrasher*," she said. "If
you get caught with it again, you'll be put on
Report."

"No, I'll be joining Foster Todd," he said, and
he passed her the magazine.

She unbuttoned her jacket and stuck it inside.
Then she began pinning her hair up. "I want to
look at it, anyway," she said. "See, your father
means well, Caleb."

"He knows how to keep me quiet so he can talk."

"He won't really take away your allowance, will he?"

Caleb laughed. "Yes, he will. I'll have to hock your watch."

"Why didn't you wear it tonight?"

"I wore this beauty he gave me, instead." Caleb shot his wrist forward to show us a Timex.

"You can wear mine indefinitely," she said.

Caleb stared out the window. He said, "I hate him!"

"Come on, Caleb," she said. "He *tried*. He couldn't have been nicer to *me*."

We walked to the fork in the hill where I turned up toward my house, and they headed down to Slaughter.

It was a clear moonlit night near ten o'clock.

A lone crow was walking a punishment tour down in The Yard — Foster Todd's roommate — on report for not turning him in when he knew there were cigarettes in his locker.

My father was walking Ike when I got in.

I went upstairs.

Fanny had left the light on in his bedroom. His pills were laid out on the Kleenex, on his bed.

I undressed down to my Jockeys and sat down at my little Mac.

Now Frankenlouse's secret was out and the other lice were laughing at him, calling him a phony, and an "onster" because he could not say *M*. He begged Sugarplum:

I fiddled with the idea for awhile, until I heard my father return.

He shouted up, "Nick? Are you in?"

"Yes, sir."

"Grandfather is still out?"

"Yes, sir. They were at the hotel."

"I'll wait up awhile."

"Sir?"

"What?"
"Grandfather said not to wait up."
"What is that supposed to mean?"
"I'm just repeating what he said, sir."
"Why would he say such a thing?"
"I don't really know, sir."
"I'm not waiting up for *him*!"
"Yes, sir."
"I'm not waiting up! I'm reading!"
"Good night, sir."
"Good night!"

I always put out my lights when the first bugler sounded taps, even though I might put them back on later. I liked to open the window and look down toward The Yard and see all the lights go out in the barracks.

When I was younger, my mother used to come into my room and sit on my bed and listen with me.

My father never stopped what he was doing. Either he was inured to the sound or, like everything else, just couldn't bring himself to show he was affected by it.

I thought of the inscription inside *Frankenstein* which my father'd written to my mother: *my love for you is monstrous.* I wondered how long ago that was and what he was like back then.

The third bugler began his taps.

I had the idea that sound would ring in my memory long after I left Blister . . . and no matter what, it'd make me miss the place.

CHAPTER TWENTY-ONE

The Boeing 757 was circling LaGuardia Airport when Kinya brought up the subject of Foster Todd's expulsion.

"Maybe the Anti-Bias Equality League will turn it around," Kinya said.

"Not a chance. ABEL can't change the facts. You know The General: He just deals with the facts."

"The General wouldn't have expelled a white guy for smoking, do you think, Nick?"

"White, black, yellow, red — he's color blind. It's the rules he's interested in, only the rules."

"He'd expel a white crow for smoking, in his last year at Blister?"

"Smoking is against the rules. I'm telling you, Kinya, he goes by the book."

"Or the book he crawled out of," Kinya snickered. "Frankenlouse the Bully."

"No. Don't confuse my cartoon with my old man."

"He inspired it."

"Part of it . . . but he's not Frankenlouse, not really."

"Don't start sticking up for him now. You got it right the first time."

"He'd have expelled *me*, if I'd been caught smoking."

"Oh, sure."

"He would have!"

Kinya slapped a copy of *Science Digest* in his briefcase, and glanced out the window. Then he looked back at me and said, "You're just chicken, Nick. You draw him the way he is, but when you don't have a pencil in your hand he's only doing his job. He wrecked Todd when Todd had only seven months to go. He'd never have done that to your pal, Caleb, for example."

"Bull! He'd love to get Caleb out!"

"But he hasn't, and he wouldn't . . . not just for smoking one cigarette! Get real, Nick!"

I was too steamed to answer him.

We sat side by side in silence, and by the time we deplaned I had a knot in my stomach.

As soon as Kinya and I walked past Security, we saw him.

You couldn't miss him.

He was as tall as Kinya was. From the neck up he looked like a rooster wearing shades, with this big beak and glossy fire-colored hair. Then came the fur coat, all the way down to his leather lace-up boots. Jeans rolled, and a black turtle-neck sweater with a large silver saber hanging on a piece of white rope.

He was carrying a handmade sign that said NICK REBER in big block letters.

Kinya said, "Who the heck is that, Nick?"

"Mom must have sent someone to pick us up."

Then he came rushing at us, grinning at me, holding out his hand. "You're Nicky, I bet! I'm Sam Saber."

I introduced Kinya, and Sam Saber told us his car was just across the street in the airport garage.

He said he recognized me from the photograph my mom had in her apartment. He was taking us to his place, he said. Kinya's father would meet him in front of the Hilton in an hour and a half.

"Did your mother tell you about me?" he asked.

"No."

"*No?* Not anything?"

"*Nada*," I said.

The first big clue to Sam Saber was the license plate on the back of his white Mercedes.

It said: N U R S E.

He wasn't one.

What he was, was a writer who wrote nurse novels.

By the time we got to his place down in Greenwich Village, Kinya and I had forgotten our argument on the plane and we were giving each other looks. I knew Kinya was dying to make a crack about the fur coat. At Blister, he was second to Aaron in touting animal rights — not a vegetarian like Aaron, but he'd signed the petition against serving veal at Mess; and he was one of the cadets responsible for Blister's switch from dead frogs to rubber ones for use in science lab.

On the ride downtown, Sam Saber taught me there were worse things than my grandfather's cigarettes: there were black Bolivian cigars, one of which hung from his mouth while he drove, as smoke filled the car along with music from a Barry Manilow tape.

While we were getting our luggage out of the car, Kinya said to me, "I haven't heard that kind of honky music since my mom took me to *Fin-*

ian's Rainbow! — My gawd, 'Mandy'!"

"And 'Copacabana'!" I said.

"And 'I Can't Smile Without You'! — you *owe* me, Nick!"

Sam Saber went off to look for a parking place, and we lugged our garment bags three flights up. There was another saber on the outside of his apartment door.

We rang the bell and Mom greeted us in a black leotard, a baggy white sweater, slim black leg warmers, and ballet slippers. Her blonde hair was spilling to her shoulders, and she had this silly grin on her face.

"How do you like Sam?" she said. "You can tell the truth."

Kinya shook her hand and said, "No comment, Mrs. Reber."

"Come on, he's not *that* bad."

We wandered around the apartment while Mom got us Cokes.

There was a wall of books at one end, a shelf of them filled with Sharon Saber Nurse Novels.

That was his pseudonym: Sharon Saber.

There was *Nurse of the North, Nurse in Trouble, Nurse of the Arctic, Nurse of the Wilderness*, on and on.

I opened one book and flipped to the last page.

I nudged Kinya and showed him the last line.

Emily Fountain buttoned her coat, walked into the starry night and thought to herself how glad she was that she was nurse of the North.

Finally, Kinya said, "It's not easy to leave these nurses, but my dad's never late, Nick."

I walked him to the door, and left him bumping his bag back down the stairs.

Mom said, "Sam's taking us to dinner, honey. At least we'll get a good meal."

I supposed that meant lugging my bag around.

I said, "Why doesn't he live somewhere with a doorman?"

"I don't have a doorman, either."

"You're not a rich and successful nurse," I said.

"You don't *dislike* him, do you?"

Sam was in his bedroom getting his messages from an answering machine.

I was busy copying down something he'd left in his typewriter.

Sam didn't use a computer. He said he couldn't warm up to one.

"Nicky?" Mom said, "I'm talking to you."

"I don't dislike him, no," I said.

"What are you writing?"

I put my notebook back in my pocket, and pointed to the sheet in the typewriter.

She read the two lines aloud: "Hop to it, Nurse Roger, and put an *e* on that hop. For hope. Because the nurse of the Andes is never without hope!"

Mom looked at me. "What do you want that for?"

"For *Frankenlouse*," I said.

"Honey, I didn't raise you to be a plagiarist!"

CHAPTER TWENTY-TWO

We walked to the restaurant, Sam with his arm around my mother.

Later, Mom said Sam never should have chosen to eat in Greenwich Village because she didn't think there would have been so much flak about his fur coat uptown.

But Sam was oblivious to it all.

To the woman who said animals didn't wear people and people shouldn't wear animals!

To the teenage boys who shouted "Hey, Killer! Where'd you get the skins?"

To the blush of embarrassment on my own face, as I tried lagging behind, as though I wasn't with them.

And to the people getting their cloth coats from the checkroom, who were giving Sam dirty looks.

When we sat down, Sam said, "The wearers

of leather shoes, belts, and watch straps look
down on the wearers of warm winter coats.
There's always someone who's not as wonderful
as you are in this universe, always a nose picker
who picks his own nose prettier than you pick
yours."

He laughed, looked pleased with himself, and
ordered two martinis and a Coke. He leaned
against my mother and told her she was beau-
tiful and he was thrilled to be with her.

I looked away. I'd never seen my mother being
seduced, certainly not by The General. Now this
man with a nose like Barbra Striesand's was nuz-
zling my mother.

When the waiter brought the order there were
two gift-wrapped boxes on the tray beside the
drinks. He put one in front of me and one in
front of my mother.

"Sam, what's going on?"said my mother.

"Open it and see."

He turned to me. "You, too, Nicky. . . . Terri,
how come you never mentioned me to Nicky?
Don't I rate at all?"

"Sure, you rate, Sam. But I was saving you as
a surprise for Nicky."

"Surprised, Nicky?" he asked me.

"You could say that." Surprised didn't cover
it. Sam was the sort people stared at even when

he didn't have his fur coat on. He was a presence. Not the way my father was — not because he was formidable, but because he was flamboyant: everything opposite to my father. A loud talker, a toucher, the type who threw his head back when he laughed and slapped his knee. A strutting rooster while my father was a watchful lion.

I couldn't look him in the eye. I was afraid he'd read my mind — see the words *what do you think you're doing with my mother*? burning through my forehead in flashing neon.

I was tearing the paper off a book. At the same time my mother gasped as she saw a tiny blue box, and she said, "Tiffany! Sam! What is this?"

It was a gold bracelet, engraved with tiny words my mother had to squint to read. " 'Silver, month, window, orange, plinth, false, depth, chimney, swamp.' "

She looked up at Sam. "I guess I'm dense."

"There's a card in the box," Sam said.

She gave him a quizzical look, then took the card out and read, " 'Just as there is no rhyme for any of these words in the English language, there is no match for you, Terri.' "

Sam reached for the bracelet. "Here. I'll put it on!"

My mother kept shaking her head as though

she was amazed, and she was blushing, but she was smiling, too.

I was trying to rhyme silver, month, window — I gave up.

I took the book out of the wrapping paper.

My Life as a Cartoonist, by Harvey Kurtzman.

"Your mother says that's what you want to be," Sam said. "I used to know Kurtzman. He started *Mad* magazine."

"Thanks, Sam," I said. My eyes said: *You can't buy your way in, either!* His blinked back: *That's what you think!*

He said, "We both graduated from the same high school. Not at the same time. Harvey was a lot older. . . . Did you ever hear of the High School of Music and Art?"

"This is Nicky's first time in New York," my mother said. "But *I've* heard of it. I didn't know you went there, Sam."

"That's where Nurse Saber got her start," he said. Then he gave my wrist a punch. "And that's where *you* should be going to school, Nicky."

CHAPTER TWENTY-THREE

My aunt Priscilla's apartment on the Upper West Side was two tiny rooms with a kitchen and bath the size of small closets.

I had to push the panty hose out of the way to shower, and I knocked over bottles of Charlie, hair spray, nail polish, and hand lotion trying to get my hands on a tube of toothpaste.

My aunt Priscilla was a L'Oreal 7½ Medium Ash Blonde vegetarian casting director, who'd spent the rest of the night, after we got in from dinner, bad-mouthing Sam Saber.

I only half listened. I was in her bedroom on the unmade bed covered with clothes and magazines, reading the Kurtzman book, and looking at his cartoons. Mickey Rodent and Superduperman from *MAD*, and Little Annie Fanny from *Playboy*.

I spent the night on a Hide-A-Bed in a room

filled with furniture, books, my aunt's bicycle, a coatrack bending from the weight of duffel coats, hats and scarves, an ironing board, and a floor filled with boots, shopping carts, mops, brooms, and a vacuum cleaner with its hose snaking around it.

I went to sleep hearing my aunt shout that she'd bet a month's rent Sam dyed his hair — it was too red — and I drifted off into a dream of seeing my own cartoons printed on a sheet of paper, being handed out in a schoolyard with fire-red slides and white rope swings.

Kurtzman had published his first cartoons in the school newspaper. Blister didn't even have one.

Sam Saber wanted to take us all out to eat Thanksgiving Day, but my mother told him she wanted to spend it quietly with me and Aunt Priscilla.

Several dozen roses arrived from Sam while my mother and I were talking in the bedroom, and Aunt Priscilla was trying to baste a turkey in the kitchen.

She had some old tapes playing on the sound system: Whitney Houston, Eric Clapton, Neil Young.

My mother and I were catching up on each

others' news, while my aunt was screaming at us to put the roses in water if we could find anything big enough to contain them.

I was telling Mom about the argument I had with Kinya on the plane, and all the flak Dad was getting from everywhere for expelling Foster Todd.

"He *expelled* the boy?" my mom said.

"You know Dad. The guy broke the rules!"

"Still," my mother said.

"Still what? It doesn't have anything to do with Foster Todd being black!"

"I know that, Nicky, but — "

"But *what*?"

She reached out and hugged me. "Nicky, don't be so rigid. Don't turn into your father before my eyes."

"I wasn't defending what he did, Mom. I was just saying that's the way Dad is about rules."

"I would have told Kinya I thought it sucked!"

"Then he'd think it was because Foster was black!"

"Oh, Nicky, it doesn't hurt to say your father was harsh, possibly even *wrong*."

"Let's not talk about it!" I said. "You don't get it! You go around with a guy in furs, for Pete's sake!"

"A guy who's thoughtful enough to think of you, Nicky!"

"Because he's got a thing for you."

"It's not a thing he's got. He's fond of me. Can't you talk about affection without being self-conscious?"

I'd had it, and I got up to go into the next room, stumbling over a pair of furry mules sticking out from under the bed. "Nobody picks up around here!" I shouted.

"That's right, General," my mother chuckled. "We're too busy having fun."

By the time Aunt Priscilla was pulling the turkey out of the oven that afternoon, I'd finished *My Life as a Cartoonist* by Harvey Kurtzman, and my mother'd read all that I'd done so far of *Frankenlouse*.

The three of us had Thanksgiving dinner on a card table in the living room, while we talked about the High School of Music and Art. Nurse Saber had reached me.

"You could live with me," Mom said. "I'll have an apartment by then."

"*Maybe*," Aunt Priscilla said.

"Hopefully," Mom said.

"Dad would never agree," I said. "*Would* he?"

"Dad isn't your only parent, Nicky. . . . If you really want to do this we have to set the ball in motion."

"And give Vesuvius time to erupt," my aunt laughed.

"You mean Frankenlouse," said my mother. . . . "Nicky, he's a wonderful character. He's not really Daddy. I thought he was going to be some vicious portrayal of your father, but he's not at all."

"He started out like him. I certainly had him in mind. But the funny thing is these characters take on lives of their own after awhile. Sometimes he's more like me than he's like Dad."

"Or maybe you're more like Dad than you think." Mom laughed.

"Anyway, Dad will think it's him if I ever show it to him."

"Don't then. Just tell him that you want to be a cartoonist, that you need an environment where you can be with others who want to be artists, where you can study art."

"Sure," Aunt Priscilla said. "Just tell him that and then run for your life."

"Oh, he's not that bad, Pris. . . . He listens to reason, sometimes."

"That's like saying sometimes C follows F or

three follows eight," my aunt said. "Patch is not known for his flexibility."

I said, "What about *my love for you is monstrous*, Mom? What was he like when he wrote that in *Frankenstein*?"

My mother looked at me. "Is that what you thought? That Daddy wrote that? Nicky, your father would *never* write that, say that, or think that. That kind of show of emotion is like the letter *M* is to Frankenlouse. I love your father, for all his faults, but that is not Daddy's style. . . . Daddy wouldn't take on anything bigger than Daddy, not *anything* monstrous."

Aunt Priscilla grinned at me. "I would, though."

"Pris gave me that book, Nick."

"Out of monstrous affection for my kid sister. . . . Who wants more turkey?"

"I do," my mother said.

"How come you married Daddy?"

"I didn't believe in myself," my mother said. "I believed more in him."

"She fell in love with the uniform," said Aunt Priscilla. "At least an Army uniform beats a nurse's."

My mother said, "No. I loved *him*. I wanted someone I could count on, and I got it. . . . It was Patch who couldn't count on me. I could never squelch this yearning I have to try and be someone in my own right."

"Do you still want to dance?" I asked her.

"I'm too old now. I don't know what I want, Nicky. I wish I'd been like you when I was your age. I wish I'd had one dream instead of a hundred."

Aunt Priscilla dropped a turkey leg on my mother's plate and sat back down at the table.

My mother said, "It's not good to be my age and still want something to happen that'll change your life. You have to plan ahead, Nick."

"Plan ahead!" my aunt said. "What movie are we going to tonight?"

"You can be what you want to be, Nick," said my mother, "but you have to take the steps toward it very carefully."

"Don't dream, *scheme*," said my aunt. "Let's go to Radio City. I love those Rockettes!"

"Not the Rockettes," my mother said. "All those young girls dancing on stage — that breaks my heart. . . . Nicky, you've got talent. You're not the type that'll be happy marching in step at West Point or anywhere else."

"It's telling Dad that's the hard part," I said.

"Telling him isn't the hard part," said my

aunt, "the hard part is getting out of his way *after* you tell him."

My mother said, "He let me go. I went."

"You're not his flesh and blood, Terri. Nick is *his* dream."

Before we left for the movies, I went into the bedroom to check in with my father and to wish him a happy Thanksgiving.

I pushed away the clothes piled on the unmade bed and sat down.

My father said, "You didn't have to call. You wished me that when you left yesterday."

"I just thought I'd call."

"Well, you have." And then he managed, "Are you enjoying yourself?"

"Yes, sir. Did you and Grandad have turkey?"

"I don't know what Grandad had. I had turkey."

"Did you eat there or — "

He cut me off. "Where would I eat? I have Thanksgiving in my own home."

I thought of him sitting at the long table with Ike right around the corner. I couldn't ask him if anyone had been there to eat with him.

"Well, sir, I'll see you Sunday night."

"As planned," he said.

"Yes, sir. As planned. . . . Well, good night, sir."

"Nick?"

"Yes?" I wondered if he was going to choke out a happy Thanksgiving to me, too.

"Don't miss your plane. If you miss curfew you'll have to go on report."

"Good night, sir," I said.

"Good night," he said.

CHAPTER TWENTY-FOUR

The week before Christmas Aaron and Jessie danced to something from Tchaikovsky, just the two of them on stage, a violin the only music.

It was part of the Saturday Night Series, held in Blister Hall, the public invited.

I went with Caleb, and Kinya went with the only other black left in the academy, Bud Gilbert, the crow who'd been Foster Todd's roommate. My father was still getting heat from ABEL, and there'd been an article in *People* magazine about "The Military School Without a Heart." The article also pointed out that my father's FFTs ended *You're at BLISTER, Mister*, leaving out the female cadets.

Unique had been in the news, too, and on a late-night talk show, where she'd said she was entering a drug rehabilitation center. She was teetering around in her high heels, wearing a necktie and a leather suit, carrying a stick with a gold star on the end of it.

Before the performance started, Caleb borrowed ten dollars from me. His father had kept his promise to dock his allowance for three months. Caleb was broke and down. He wanted to enter the big skateboard competition with Augusta Military Academy, but he didn't even have the bus fare to go over there for practice.

"Borrow from Jessie next time," I said. "I'm trying to save. She'd love to lend you dough."

"I can't stand her, Nick! She stares at me, follows me, and even saves the paper napkins I use at Mess!"

"Did you give her back her watch?"

"Not yet."

"Caleb, why are you so hung up on that watch?"

"It's not her. It's Skintight! He brings me luck."

"You don't even know him."

"But I'm going to. Someday. And I'm going to do what he did. Go professional. Get someone to sponsor me. He got sponsored when he was my age."

"But then he got out of skateboarding and went with Filthy Lucre!"

"Still — he did it. I just want to do it! . . .

What about you? Did you tell your dad about that high school in New York yet?"

"He's getting too much flak from ABEL now."

"You keep waiting and it'll be too late."

"I told my grandfather."

"And?"

"He said I should go to West Point first."

"What a surprise."

Then the lights dimmed and the performance started.

Aaron was alone on stage, kneeling and curled. Jessie made her entrance. Her hair was down her back. She was all in white and he was all in black.

I sat and thought through things like that.

The Jessie dancing on stage so passionately with Aaron was a far cry from the Jessie my father'd told me about when I got back from New York.

He'd invited her to have Thanksgiving with him, the crow whose family was in Egypt, and some faculty, but she'd chosen to eat at Mess, where Caleb ate.

My father didn't tell me it was because of Caleb. I knew that.

My father thought it was Aaron who had a "hold" on her.

He said he saw them everywhere together on

the base, and that was true. Aaron was her
sounding board. Aaron had to listen endlessly
to her chatter about Caleb: every boring little
detail of Caleb's daily life from what he was
putting on his zits to what tricks he was doing
on his skateboard. She had the whole vocabu-
lary, and even knew the ledges he waxed for his
backside tailslides, and every time he broke a
deck.

I'd run into her a few times and gotten my
own fill of it. I couldn't wait to get away. But
Aaron had the patience of Job with her.

My father said Jessie's grades were slipping.
She was referred to Lieutenant Leslie for coun-
seling because she was crying herself to sleep
some nights. My father blamed Unique. When
I said I didn't think she gave a damn about
Unique — she never even mentioned Unique —
he said to repeat those last five words and that
ought to tell me something about that poor child.
He gave me a look: You don't really think she
can just ignore a mother like that? And she's all
Jessie has, Nick!

I only knew Jessie made me feel sorry for her.
I wasn't my father's son when that happened.
He'd sweat it but I'd duck it. They weren't my
troops. I had to look out for what was going
down in my own life, and sweat that.

I thought about my mother's latest letter telling me the same thing Caleb had just said: It'd be too late if I kept waiting. *Tell your father straight out!*

Mom's letters always ended "Sam sends love."

She'd been so starved for love she'd wound up with a man in mink who smoked smelly cigars and paid extra for vanity license plates.

At last I'd gotten something from Sam for my cartoon strip — a song the lice sing as they joyfully continue with plans for their Hop, no longer afraid of the "onster."

LIFT UP YOUR LEGS AND HOP!
HIPPETY, HIPPETY HOP,
JUST STICK AN "E" ON HOP, SEE?
YOU'VE GOT HOPE AS YOU HOP,
AS YOU HOP,
YOU'VE GOT H O P EEEE!

While the audience applauded and Aaron and Jessie took their bows, I made up my mind to tackle my own situation that very night . . . I'd head home early. I'd snare the lion in his den, while my grandfather was seeing Heavy Meadow home.

On the way out of Blister Hall, Kinya gave me a brief glance, but he was chilled ever since our plane ride to New York. The Foster Todd thing was still smoldering.

I walked with Caleb as far as Slaughter.

"What they ought to do with Jessie," he said, "is lock her in a box and only let her out to dance. When she's not up on her toes, she's a mess."

"Give her back her watch," I said.

"I may have to pawn it," he said. "I could, you know. I could do anything to that girl and she'd just stare at me with those startled-fawn-in-the-headlights eyes!"

"Wish me luck," I said, "I'm going to confront himself tonight."

Caleb gave my back a slap. "Sic 'em, boy!"

If I believed God really had time for Nick Reber of Blister Military Academy, I'd have suspected He was pushing for me to have a West Point education, too.

I'd have blamed Him for the fate awaiting me when I walked through my front door with everything I was going to say about a career in cartooning on the tip of my tongue.

Poison had arrived by limousine in her cat box from the Old Dominion Airport.

A note from Unique explained that she was only to stay with Jessie for one month.

Time is too short for me to make other plans. With love. U.

My father had gotten in before me. His braided cap was on the hall table next to the other kitty, the one I paid into when I broke house rules.

He was racing around with the full fruit salad pinned on his uniform, muttering and snapping his fingers as though someone would jump out of the floorboards and make what was in our foyer disappear.

"Dad," I said, "you've got to take her out of the box!"

"I haven't got to do anything!" he splutterd.

At least Ike was enjoying himself, wagging his tail in fond recognition of his old buddy with her nose pressed against the airholes.

CHAPTER
TWENTY-FIVE

FOOD FOR THOUGHT

HALCYON DAYS.

The word halcyon (pronounced HAL-see-un) is an adjective meaning happy/unruffled. It is the Greek for a kingfisher who laid its eggs on the surface of the sea and incubated for fourteen days before the winter solstice, when the waves were always calm and unruffled.

These are *your* halcyon days — your days at Blister, before you leave us to take your place in the larger world.

You will always look back upon them as the best of times.

But do not wait until then to appreciate what you have now: the friends you're making, the lessons you're learning, the goals you are setting for yourselves.

You are in an environment that nourishes you and prepares you for tomorrow.

You're at BLISTER, Mister!

Or Ms. — as the case may be.

MERRY CHRISTMAS!

CHAPTER TWENTY-SIX

Poison was returned to us after a trial period with Heavy Meadow.

Every inch of her Siamese self had rebuffed the lieutenant, and to escape her she scaled draperies and scooted under beds, hissing and swiping at her.

In our house she was content, sleeping with Ike inside his cedar bag, seeking out sunspots to stretch out in, or clawing on the arm of my father's upholstered armchair.

Now whenever my father entered the living room he could be counted on to say the same four words the moment he set eyes on her. *She has to go!*

But she was still with us on Christmas Day, as Caleb was, the Little Soldier from Costa Rica, a crow named Harvey Holmquist whose parents were archaeologists off somewhere in Egypt and, of course, Jessie.

Jessie wasn't interested in Poison, and she felt no particular gratitude to my father for not shipping the cat off to the nearest animal shelter.

Before Aaron went home for the holidays he checked on the cat daily, and he left a catnip mouse for her Christmas gift, which Poison gutted immediately.

Fanny served us all a standing rib roast with mashed potatoes, gravy, string beans, and salad. We had cake and ice cream after that.

"I thought the evening went very well," said my father after everyone left.

"We tried, anyway," I said, because I always felt sorry for the ones who had nowhere to go. "Why didn't Grandfather come with Lieutenant Meadow?"

"Because of that animal!" my father barked. "Lieutenant Meadow is convinced that cat has it in for her!"

We were upstairs.

My father was in his pajamas. He had just taken his pills and gargled. It was near time for taps, which was played on tape since our buglers were on leave along with everyone else.

I was standing in my shorts, in the doorway of my bedroom.

"Could I say something to you, sir?"

"What?" He was standing in the doorway of his bedroom.

"I would like to be a cartoonist," I said.

"What?"

"I've been wanting to tell you that I'd like to be a cartoonist."

He said, "You'll outgrow that. I once thought I wanted to be a photographer. I was about your age. I had a new camera and — "

I interrupted him. "This isn't something I'll outgrow. Could we talk about it?"

"Now?"

"If you don't mind, sir. I have to make plans."

"What do you mean you have to make plans?"

"Could we talk somewhere besides here in the hall?"

"Where should we talk?" He was rattled; this was an unscheduled maneuver. He looked around as though there was some conference room he hadn't remembered, where we could put this matter on the table and deal with it.

"You want to come in my room?" I said.

"All right. In your room," he said.

"It's not picked up in here," I said.

He said, "Well, it's Christmas."

He went across to my desk chair and I sat down on my bed.

"What is this all about, Nick?"

I told him everything. I could hear taps play somewhere in the middle, but if it registered with him, his face didn't show it. He sat there with the kind of expression I'd expect him to have if I was telling him I had a $500-a-month crack habit.

At the end I told him about the Kurtzman book, and the High School of Music and Art in New York City, and Mom's suggestion that I live with her.

Then I waited for Vesuvius to erupt.

Instead, he shook his head and said, "I'm surprised at you, Nick. I'm very surprised."

"I knew you would be."

"Do you know why?"

"Because you always thought I'd graduate from Blister and then go on to West Point."

"That's isn't why," he said. "I'll tell you why. I think of cartoons and I think of what you see in cartoons."

"*Sir?*" I said. I couldn't even imagine him thinking of cartoons, but The General was a hid-

den man. You never knew what he'd come up
with.

"I think of your average cartoon," he said. "I
think of what you see. You see people stranded
on desert islands. You see prisoners trying to
escape from their cells. You see people on
beds of nails. You know what you see in cartoons."

"I never thought of that," I said. I hadn't.

He looked pleased, as though he'd pointed
out something to me that would make the whole
notion of cartooning disappear.

He said, "You see people on ledges about
to jump and you see people on psychiatrists'
couches. You know what you see."

"What are you saying, sir?" I asked him.

"I'm saying that isn't you, Nick. You're not in
some desperate situation."

"Those aren't the only situations in cartoons,
Dad."

"But those are major themes, Nick. They're
recurring themes. . . . People who draw cartoons
are all bogged down in paranoid thinking: paranoid, masochistic thinking. . . . And how many
female cartoonists are there?"

"Not a lot," I said.

"No, because women don't have that negative
streak some men do."

I just sat there. It reminded me of his argument against skateboarding. It was *where* they skated that bothered him. Backs of places and behind things: never out in the open.

I just looked at him.

"You're not a negative thinker, Nick."

"I *wasn't*," I agreed, "but I could be, with a few more conversations like this."

"This isn't a time to wisecrack, Nick."

"Dad, sir, I'm trying to tell you something I want to be, and you're analyzing the kind of people who do what I want to do."

"What do you expect me to do?"

"What if I analyze the kind of people who go to West Point? What if I say they're war-lovers or people whose parents make them go there, or automatons who just want to follow orders?"

My father smiled. He said, "How about pa-triots? How about men who want to accept responsibility?"

"Very few women go to West Point, so they must be unpatriotic and irresponsible."

He shook his head. "Nicky, Nicky, don't try to twist my meaning. . . . This is your mother's idea, isn't it?"

"No, it's my idea."

"It's your idea to leave Blister and go live in

New York? Go to some sissy high school where they dance and draw all day?'' He was getting steamed.

I said, ''Being interested in the arts isn't a sissy idea, Dad.''

''I take that back. But not the rest.''

Then he stood up. ''I think we should both cool off before we discuss this any further.''

I didn't need to cool off. I couldn't have felt cooler.

''We have to deal with it, soon,'' I said. ''I have to put in an application for that school.''

''Did you leave the door unlocked for your grandfather?''

''Yes, sir.''

''I'm going to turn in, Nick.''

''I see that,'' I said.

''Good night,'' he said.

I didn't answer him.

He started out of the room and paused in the doorway.

He said, ''Not that there are not good cartoonists. There are good cartoonists. Trudeau, Ernie Pyle from World War II, Herblock. . . . But these men are commenting on the real world out there . . . and you have to have some experience to do that. Maybe after West Point, if you still want to — ''

I said, "I don't want to go to West Point. I don't want to wait until I finish here. I want to go to that high school in New York next year."

"Your mother is a very selfish woman," he said. "She's not thinking of your future."

Then he tramped down the hall and slammed his door.

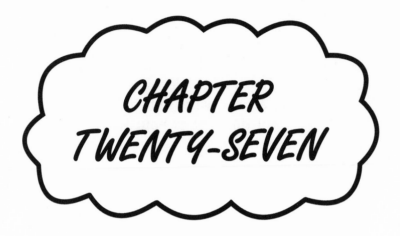

CHAPTER TWENTY-SEVEN

Frankenlouse was turning into me: wanting out now, hating the feeling of being trapped in a place where he didn't feel he belonged. ("If I could just ake it out of here and find y way ho e!)

I didn't know how I was going to get him back to the horror library where he belonged. For myself, I filled out the application my mother mailed to me for the High School of Music and Art.

I wrote your father a strong letter about this, she wrote me. *Has he mentioned it to you?*

He didn't say anything to me.

Life went on as usual in our house, except for the fact that my grandfather was hardly ever home, and Poison had decided her favorite spot was my father's armchair.

He would come home, find her hairs there,

and cuss — a rare show of emotion from The General, who had always taught Blister cadets that such language was the last resort of mediocre personalities.

I didn't rub it in. I decided to hit the books hard so he couldn't blame poor grades on this masochistic and paranoid personality who wanted to make his living drawing cartoons. I kept my distance while I nourished the dream, talking about it only with Caleb.

By the time he had his allowance back he owed every cadet in Blister. He was doing yard work for Heavy Meadow to pay off his debts. He had pawned his Walkman and a gold ring left him by his mother, but he was still a few hundred bucks behind.

One day after classes, I went over to Slaughter to see him, just in time for the blowup that had been in the making ever since Jessie Southgate had arrived.

If I didn't know that she often cried herself to sleep, I'd think she had ice running through her veins because of the way she shrugged her shoulders and said she didn't care what we did with the cat at Christmas . . . and because of her reaction when Caleb began shouting at her that afternoon.

I'd walked in on it at its pitch, in time to see

him slap the watch down on the table in the front parlor.

A lot of the Little Soldiers were in the rec room nearby watching an old rerun of *The Cosby Show* on TV. The sound got turned down soon, and you could see other worms coming down the stairway to see what the shouting was all about.

Caleb called her a pathetic little wretch with a slut for a mother and a dummy for a best friend. He said her crush on him made him want to barf, and he said she had to be a major dork not to know everyone laughed at her behind her back. On and on.

Jessie just sat there with this crooked smile on her face, polishing the brass on her garrison belt as though she hadn't heard anything he said, and wasn't even aware of the commotion he'd caused in Slaughter.

I grabbed Caleb and got him out of there before the house officers heard him.

Caleb said, "She didn't react because she *loved* it! She was dying for me to crack! That way she knows she got to me!"

"She got to you, all right."

"Haven't you noticed she doesn't react to anything major? Nothing! Her mother could climb the flagpole in front of the White House naked and she'd just go along like it was another day, but if the wind blows my hair to the left she swoons and says she loves my hair blowing that way and would I like to read the poem she wrote about it!"

"Calm down," I said.

I got him to sit on the stone bench near The Yard until he caught his breath and could fill me in on what had triggered his rage.

She hadn't done anything that bad. She'd taken a pair of clean socks from his drawer to keep under her pillow. But he'd found out about it at the same time he'd heard there was a hundred dollar registration fee for the skateboard competition with Augusta. And that morning a video from his father had arrived telling him he was being enrolled in a language camp for the summer, since his worst grades were in Spanish and French.

The best thing about Caleb was he could be obsessed with skateboarding, driven crazy by Jessie, picked on by his old man, and one report away from expulsion at Blister, but he still thought to ask me how I was doing.

"I'm going ahead with my plans," I said. "The General's not dealing with it."

"How's he taking the news about your grandfather and Heavy Meadow?"

"What news? They're not news anymore."

"She told me I could paint her front porch Valentine's weekend, because she's getting married."

That was the first I heard about it.

When I got home that night Poison was on our front porch in her cat box, because Heavy Meadow was in the living room with my grandfather, breaking the news to The General.

I went around to the kitchen door so I could sneak up the backstairs. But I could hear my father's voice loud and clear. "Of course I'm pleased!" he was shouting. "You don't think I want my old man underfoot telling me he knows a better way to do everything!"

"Well, he *does*!" my grandfather laughed.

Lieutenant Meadow's voice was on edge, too. She said, "He wanted to recite Longfellow's 'Hiawatha's Wooing' before we take our marriage vows and I said nothing doing!"

"Longfellow — Ho! Ho!" — my father said.

"What's wrong with that? Ha! Ha!" My grandfather asked.

Ha-ha and hee-hee, I thought. The three of them sounded like strangers in an elevator, forced to talk by some calamity.

CHAPTER TWENTY-EIGHT

When my father really hated something that was happening to him, but knew there was nothing he could do about it, he acted sappy.

The day he drove my mother to the airport he was whistling under his breath in the car, and pointing out the cows sitting down in the pastures, saying it was a sign of rain. . . . Clapping his hands together, while the three of us waited at the departure gate, he shuffled his feet, grinned, and said things like they'd done a good job building the new terminal, that Old Dominion could be proud of itself etcetera, etcetera. A lot of blather to cover up the fact his wife was leaving him and it'd hit him like a ton of bricks.

I think what bothered him most about my grandfather marrying Heavy Meadow was that my grandfather was beginning a whole new life, and my father was still watching his come apart at the seams.

He didn't say that. He bounded around the house the evening of the wedding checking on the flowers and humming to himself, something he never did, and he talked to Ike about being a good dog when the guests arrived, something he never did. Ike was watching him uncertainly, tail half-raised, almost wagging, but suspicious of the lighthearted behavior, as I was of the friendly banter, and his drink of whiskey (something he rarely drank) before people started arriving.

Poison was upstairs in my room.

The wedding was to take place in our living room, in front of the fireplace, at seven P.M. or 1900 hours as my father put it.

Heavy Meadow was going to come down the staircase from my mother's sewing room, and take my father's arm, since he was giving her away.

My mother called to wish my grandfather luck, and I spoke with her.

"How's your father doing?" she asked.

"He keeps saying, 'This is a wonderful day.' "

"He's taking it that bad, hmmm?"

"Yeah. And since they're moving to Tucson, he has to find a new English teacher."

"That surprises me," said my mother. "I thought they'd live at Blister and she'd keep on teaching."

"Dad keeps saying, 'Arizona's not that far away!'"

"Be gentle with him, Nicky. Don't push New York right now."

"I haven't been."

"Sam sends love."

"Don't keep telling me that. I don't even know him."

"Okay," she said. "Have it your way. He's sending you his latest. It's called *Nurse of the Highlands*." She chuckled.

I said, "I don't want it!"

"You two are going to be basket cases living in that big house all alone. You may want some nursing tips. . . . Bye, honey. Enjoy the wedding!"

After everyone was gathered around the living room, my father thanked them for coming and said it was a wonderful day for what I hoped was the last time, and then one of the Little Soldiers sang "Yours Is My Heart Alone."

My father stood at the bottom of the staircase, and Heavy Meadow began her descent toward the end of the second verse.

All that we could figure out later was that once Heavy Meadow was upstairs in our house, she must have opened the wrong door while she was looking for the sewing room. She must have opened my bedroom door.

For descending with her on the staircase was Poison, who charged ahead of her, straight down into the wedding guests. In a panic at the crowd, she scaled the bookcase, knocking down a shelfful of my father's biographies of famous generals and his twelve-volume encyclopedia of military strategies, before she found her footing atop Winston Churchill's writings, where she perched, ruff up, back arched, hissing down at us.

"Still and all," my father said, when everyone was gone, "it was a wonderful day."

"Yes, sir."

He was sitting in his armchair, in his dress uniform, having a cup of coffee. He'd had the one whiskey and a glass of champagne while he toasted the happy couple, and that was all he needed to go on red alert that he might lose control. (I'd never seen him do it yet.)

He had a copy of *Vietnam Journal* on his lap, which he said Captain Tuttle had loaned him, and he'd forgotten about until Poison's leap sent it sailing to the floor.

"It doesn't belong in my library," he said gruffly. "I never approved of the way that war was fought, or *wasn't* fought," he added.

"I know that, sir."

"Yes. You know that about me. Tuttle will want this back," he said, and then he said, "I've been thinking about this cartooning you want to do, Nick."

I sat down on the couch, brushing off rice that had been thrown around the room. There was a bright half moon through the window, a starry night out there.

"What were you thinking, sir?"

"I've been thinking that I am the past and you are the present."

"Sir?"

"I've been thinking that your grandfather and I never really got along. That's probably why he got himself married and now why he's going all the way to Arizona to live. He was the past and I was the present."

I couldn't figure out what he wanted to say.

I said, "What has this to do with me and cartooning?"

"It was Winston Churchill who said if there's a quarrel between the past and the present, there's no future. He said that in a speech before the House of Commons, June, 1940."

"Yes, sir."

"So I'm not going to quarrel with you, Nick. If you want to do this thing that badly, this cartoon thing, I'm not going to let it come between us and cause a breach."

"Do you mean that, Dad?"

"If it's what you want. If you want to go and live in New York City with your mother, do it."

"Thanks, sir! Thanks, Dad!"

"It doesn't mean I approve of cartooning as a career."

"I realize that, Dad."

"And I don't think you'll like New York."

"Maybe not, sir," I said.

"So if you change your mind," he said, and he was getting up now, ready to go up to bed, "you can always come back to Blister." He picked up Tuttle's book.

"I know that, sir."

"At any time," he said. "Well, good night, Nick. I'm turning in."

That was when taps began.

I saw him pause a moment, stop, as though he had forgotten something or had more to say, but perhaps like me he was listening to the bugle sound.

Then he proceeded, and I stayed until the third and final wail, when he was already upstairs in his bathrom, gargling.

CHAPTER
TWENTY-NINE

No school had ever beaten Augusta in the skateboard competition. The Plank Pilots were the top team anywhere in the U.S.

It was my father's idea to lend Caleb the $100 registration fee, so he could be part of Blister's team.

"I'm not doing it for Caleb," my father said.

We were having breakfast together, at the same time my grandfather, back from his honeymoon, was carrying boxes from our house to Lieutenant Meadow Reber's.

"I would love to see our Yard Bombers beat their Plank Pilots," my father said.

"Caleb's better than any of them," I told him.

"So you say, and so says the coach. . . . I don't understand Peter Purr at all. This is probably the only event where Caleb can distinguish himself."

"Peter Purr hates Caleb, Dad."

My father shook his head vigorously, as though he was shaking off flies. "A man doesn't hate his own son. And when I called him to ask if he had any objections to Caleb's entering the competition, he said he was delighted."

"Why didn't you ask him to pay the fee?"

"I told him we were loaning him the money for it, and he said Caleb got an adequate allowance, and Caleb had to be responsible for his own debts. I understand that. These children of celebrities often take advantage of their situations."

"How about the celebrities taking advantage of the children's situation?" I said.

My father grunted, "That, too."

Even as we were speaking, Poison was on my father's armchair. Ike was running around in circles in the living room, not daring to bark, but unable to contain himself while the cat rolled around on the forbidden furniture.

I knew my father probably knew the cat was there, too.

Neither of us commented on the inroads the cat was making in our house. . . . She had just arrived in *Frankenlouse*, too, where she would ultimately be the one to ruin The Great Louse Hop.

> IT MAKES ITS APPROACH, AND IT IS NOT A ROACH.
> IT IS BIGGER THAN THAT, AND IT IS NOT A RAT.'
> O MY SOUL, IT'S A CAT! SOMEONE TELL IT TO SCAT!

> SCAT!
> SCAT!

After he finished his breakfast my father said, "Make it clear to Caleb that this *is* a loan."

I said I would. I didn't know how Caleb was going to pay back all that he owed.

Now he did not even have Jessie to bail him out.

Finally, she was indifferent to him. Indifferent to all of us except Aaron.

He still came by to check on Poison and brush her, never when we could see him. He either came after Retreat when we were eating, or at odd moments during the day. Fanny told me about it.

We were about to push ourselves away from the table when my grandfather called in, "Poison's on your chair, Patch!"

Ike found the courage to let out one sharp bark at the cat's name.

All my father said was, "Ike! Quiet!"

Caleb was elated when I gave him the news outside Tuttle's class.

Then he said, "You should have been at Slaughter this morning. All these flowers arrived, enough for a major funeral, and balloons, too, all from Unique to Jessie. She walked right by them, didn't even read the card. It was stuck in the middle of these white roses and it said, 'Honey, I'm okay now, almost finished with rehab, love from Mama!' "

"My father says it's a *loan*, Caleb."

"I know that. I've got an idea where I'm going to get some extra money. Don't worry. Is he going to make you pay back the money if I don't?"

"He's not your father, Caleb. That would be something your father would do."

"Right. . . . You're getting along better with him now, hmm? Ever since he said you can go to New York."

"We manage," I said.

My father had not mentioned cartooning or New York since the night of my grandfather's wedding.

"I can't believe he's going to sit somewhere and cheer for me!" Caleb said.

"He's not. He says he can't leave Blister that day, but I'm going."

"You'd better, Nick!"

It was two weeks away.

All of Blister was excited about the contest because Augusta beat us at everything, even football, which was the one sport BAM excelled at.

Suddenly, Blister's hopes were riding on Caleb Purr.

Even Dragonbreath Tuttle didn't blow a gasket when Caleb could only come up with two of Newton's three laws of motion that morning.

Caleb left out the law of inertia.

All Tuttle said was that he hoped Caleb would be a body in motion when we went up against AMA, and not a body at rest. Then he looked at the class with this sneaky little grin, as though he was expecting cheers from the cadets for getting off a good one.

I felt great about everything that night as I headed home through The Yard, while the Little Soldiers marched behind me.

We're marching smart,
Left right left right,
We take the flag down
Every night!
We're worms right now,
And so it goes,
But someday we'll
Be Blister crows!

I stood at attention with my Frankenlouse notebook at my feet, my hand over my heart, and watched the flag come down.

The bugles blew Retreat.

I could see other cadets stopped in their tracks at various spots near The Yard, waiting for the flag to be folded, and the worms to carry it away.

I didn't see Lieutenant Meadow Reber behind me until she spoke my name as soon as the bugle stopped.

She was in uniform, looking more like her old self than a new bride, even to the stern expression on her face.

But I smiled and said, "I hope you have room for everything Grandad's moving into your house."

She didn't smile back.

She said, "Your father won't be home for dinner."

That was like saying Old Faithful in Yellowstone Park couldn't be counted on to erupt. I was going to make some crack along those lines but the look in her eyes made me stop, and then made me fear something had happened to him.

I said, "Is he all right?"

"He's fine . . . considering."

"Considering what?" My heart started pounding. I was thinking about his heart, about Fanny always making sure he ate carefully because of his cholesterol. My mind was spinning with dire possibilities. Who, besides Fanny, had been looking out for him, anyway?

"This morning Jessie Southgate reported her gold watch missing, Nick," said Heavy Meadow. "This afternoon it was found hidden away down under Caleb's civies, in his duffel bag."

"Who went through his duffel bag?" That was all I could think to say. I knew as well as any cadet at Blister that house officers in Slaughter were privileged to search the duffels whenever they chose to.

"That's beside the point, Nick."

Then I thought of Caleb telling me that morning that he'd thought of a way to make money.

"Your father's at an emergency meeting of

BAM officers. I was heading over to tell you and Fanny. You'd better eat without him. He'll be very late.''

Who could eat?

I said, ''What's going to happen?''

''What do *you* think?'' she said. ''Caleb doesn't have any reports left.''

Then she gave me a two-fingered salute, the new, shiny wedding ring on one of the fingers, and that small, slanted smile of hers, which looked wistful but resigned.

CHAPTER THIRTY

"I'd like to talk to him," I said.

My father said, "You can't. He's in isolation until we go through with the court-martial."

"Had he admitted it?"

"Nick, he doesn't have to admit it! It was right there in his duffel bag! . . . He's pawned things before, you know. The same upperclassmen that buy him *Thrasher* take things in to Old Dominion and pawn them for him. A Sony Walkman, for instance. A gold ring, for instance. I just found out both things were pawned for him by Cadet Carlson."

"Is Caleb going to be expelled?"

"What choice do we have? This is so typical of Caleb," said my father, flinging his briefcase on the couch. "He flirts with trouble every time he's a little ahead. He wants to fail, Nick! The very day he got off his very last report, he showed up for our Halloween party dressed as Collateral Damage! He knew that wouldn't go over well with us! . . . And now we were putting our faith in him for the competition with AMA — and what did *he* do?"

"He was probably just trying to repay *you*," I said.

"So it's my fault, is it?"

"Why couldn't we have just *given* him the money? He was going to represent Blister!"

"Nick, the rule has always been that students pay their own fees in these competitions. Rules are rules. Caleb stole a watch! We do not, and we never will, tolerate thievery!"

"What if he didn't take that watch?" I said.

My father pushed Poison out of his chair. "He took it, Nick. Face it. Your friend has been on a downhill course ever since he arrived at Blister. . . . Do you think I like having a second student expelled? Do you think it makes Blister look good to have two students expelled in one year?"

"What if Jessie planted it there?" I persisted. "He told her off a few weeks ago! What if she's getting even?"

My father sighed. "That little girl tried to save him, for your information. She tried to say she'd loaned him the watch once they found it in his room. She tried to convince us she'd forgotten that she loaned it to him."

"Maybe she did forget," I said, but I was running out of air — and conviction.

I was glad when my father said he didn't want to discuss it anymore.

I went up to my room.

I took Ike with me for something to hold on to.

Before taps, Kinya called to tell me he was sorry about Caleb. He said, "If there's anything I can do . . . ," and his voice trailed off. He knew there wasn't.

CHAPTER THIRTY-ONE

The cruelty of Blister is the waiting when you're up for court martial, and what you're made to do while you wait.

As we walked to classes the next morning, Caleb walked a punishment tour in The Yard.

The first thing I did was seek out Jessie. I found her coming from the faculty bathroom, where she was changing after gym.

It was the very spot where I'd first introduced myself to her. She was holding her cap under her arm, exactly as she'd done that day, pinning up her hair, still damp from the shower.

"Hello, Nick. Were you waiting for someone?"

"For you, Jessie. I want to talk to you about Caleb."

"What is there to say?"

"Do you know anything I don't know, Jessie?"

"Did he send you, Nick?"

"How could he send me? I haven't been able to get near him since this whole thing happened."

"I tried to cover for him, Nick."

"So my father said."

We both stood there then. I was waiting for her to say something: maybe break down and admit she'd set Caleb up. If I could just get her to do that there'd still be time to clear Caleb.

She said, "He's going to be expelled, isn't he?"

"Jessie, he's got one foot out the door right now."

"I was telling Aaron I guess I'll never know what got into Caleb. That watch didn't mean anything to me. I would have given it to him if he'd asked. Well, you know how Caleb is."

"What do you mean I know how Caleb is? What does that mean, Jessie?"

"Caleb would never stoop to ask me for anything, would he? He certainly doesn't need a pathetic little wretch with a slut for a mother . . . oh, and a dummy for a best friend. I told that one to Aaron. I said, Aaron, it's incredible, isn't it, when you were so close to someone and then it just falls to pieces and gross things get said no one means? But still they hurt."

"Is that what this is all about, Jessie?"

"What this is all about is Caleb finally went

too far. You knew he would someday, Nick.
Everyone knew he would. Where will he go?"

"To Maine. Until his father sends him somewhere else."

She had her hair up, and she put on her cap.
The five-minute bell rang.

She said, "I'm really very, very sorry for him.
Very! You tell him that when you see him, or
write him. Okay?"

She began walking fast then, ahead of me, not
looking back.

CHAPTER THIRTY-TWO

A moment after they blew Retreat that night, Caleb was escorted to the airport by Captain Flagg, second in command at the academy.

There was no chance for me to tell him good-bye.

That week my father was busy interviewing candidates for the position that would be open in the English department after Heavy Meadow left.

Poison had fished a chicken bone out of the garbage and been rushed to the vet to have it retrieved from inside her.

The night that happened Fanny showed me a note Aaron left on the kitchen table, addressed to me.

Please get in touch with me about Poison.

I walked over to Patton Barracks after classes

next day, still down because of Caleb, not even buoyed by my mother's phone call saying Sam had found her a great apartment in the Village, with a small utility room that could be turned into a second bathroom.

The only upbeat side to our conversation was her suggestion that I invite Caleb to spend a weekend in New York with us in the summer.

My father'd said I could call him, but to wait a month. He felt Caleb needed at least that much time to distance himself from Blister, and me. He said by then I could probably give him the news that, without him, The Yard Bombers had been victorious, too.

Patton was where the crows lived. You had to go through all this rigmarole to enter there.

"Call out your name!"

"Reber, Nick."

"State your business!"

"My business is with Bindle, Aaron."

"Permission granted. Proceed Cadet."

"Cadet Reber proceeding!"

Aaron was sitting at his desk, his thick black hair combed back, the jacket to his dress uniform on the back of his chair, a crisp white shirt on with the dark blue BAM necktie.

He worked his voice machine with a small penlight, beaming it at letters which after a pause would assemble themselves into words. The sound was a reedy robot's tone without nuance or inflection.

"Come in. I've been waiting for you."

"The cat's okay, Aaron." I started to sit on his bed and the robot said, "No. In the chair. Opposite me, please."

I supposed that made it easier for his machine to work. I wasn't certain. So I sat opposite him.

"Listen, please. This is prepared."

I expected a long complaint about leaving chicken bones where a cat could reach them, and I crossed my legs and my arms and waited.

This is what the machine said next.

"I put the watch in Caleb's duffel bag. This is my *Mea Culpa*, given to you on this date for disciplinary action. Faculty already advised. Flag already at half-mast."

I stared at him.

He nodded back.

I jumped up and looked out the window.

In The Yard, on the pole, under the American flag was the light blue crow flag at half-mast, as it always was when a crow was being court-martialed.

CHAPTER THIRTY-THREE

Aaron left Blister in the early morning before the sun was up, when the sky was the light blue of our school uniforms. Someone had already raised the flags — both the crow flag and the American, at half-mast.

In full uniforms, the crows assembled and stood at the curb as Aaron got into the taxi. They sang that strange song of theirs, holding their caps over their hearts.

> *Farewell, good-bye, and so it goes,*
> *Ta-rum!*
> *And where it ends, God only knows!*
> *Ta-rum! Ta-rum!*

What was done to Caleb was undone in time for us to win the skateboarding competition with Augusta. For a reward, my father said Caleb

could move into Bradley Barracks. Out of
Slaughter and away from Jessie, I thought.

Kinya and I helped Caleb move his stuff across
the yard, on dollies we found in the new science
lab, where, thanks to Aaron (and Kinya, too),
even the worms were rubber ones.

No one believed that Aaron Bindle had set
Caleb up for a fall, and then felt so guilty he had
put in his *Mea Culpa*.

What we all believed, and could never prove,
was that Jessie put her watch in Caleb's duffel
bag, and Aaron knew it.

He may have known it at the time of Caleb's
expulsion, or he may have been told later by
Jessie. But Aaron, however he found it out,
could not bear injustice.

And Aaron was Jessie's protector.

Whatever Jessie did, Aaron defended.

My father read every report again and again
for weeks after, clinging to the idea he would
find something that could reverse matters. There
was nothing but hearsay: speculation that it
would have been impossible for someone like
Aaron to enter Slaughter without being seen by
anyone there, that he had a full class schedule
that day which took him far away from Slaugh-

ter, that he was at the dance studio when he claimed to have planted the watch, on and on.

But a *Mea Culpa* was a *Mea Culpa*.

Never in the history of Blister has a cadet ever given one when he was innocent of what he confessed to. Only Aaron could take it back, and if he did, blame would have to go somewhere. . . . We all knew where.

"I'll never believe it," my father kept repeating.

But rules were rules.

The system was the sytem.

A followed *B*, one followed two, straight ahead, straight ahead.

And Jessie Southgate?

I had one conversation with her near the end of April in a pouring rain. Both of us were under umbrellas in The Yard.

"Do you miss Aaron?" I asked her.

"Of course I miss him. He was my best friend. There's no one to partner me now in dance class, either."

"Were you surprised at his *Mea Culpa*?"

She couldn't look me in the eye. She said, "Aaron just wanted to get out of here! He never belonged here! His mother *made* him come here, because she didn't want him to be a dancer. But he *is* a dancer, and there's nothing she can do about it! He'll go to New York and dance, like his father did!''

I said, ''He could have waited until June, don't you think? Why wouldn't he wait another three months, Jessie?''

''How do I know? It isn't exactly as though he confided in me. He never did. Even if he *could* speak, I think he'd *choose* to be dumb. He's mysterious. He enjoys being mysterious!''

''Aaron didn't even like Caleb. He wouldn't take the blame for Caleb. But he would for *you*.''

I stared hard at her. I wanted her to feel me just looking at her. Both our faces were wet. Both of us had on the red rubber BAM boots as we stood in a huge puddle.

She finally said, ''I know what everybody's saying about me. Let them talk! The only reason Caleb is getting away with this is because of that competition. That's how he got himself moved to Bradley Barracks, too! I suppose he's the big hero now! But Caleb did it! Aaron's stupid — or something.''

''How about protective?''

''Of me?'' She tried to laugh but she sounded breathless and close to tears. ''I don't need protection! What from? I don't need this place, either, and I won't be back next year!" Then she seemed to pull herself together. She straightened her shoulders, and this time managed a small, mocking laugh. "All these meaningless rules, Nick! Some of us don't really belong in places with all these meaningless rules. Like who *needs* it? Right?"

I thought of that early evening we walked down to the hotel to meet Caleb's father, how innocent she seemed then, and how she'd asked me if she looked pretty.

"What *do* you care about, Jessie?" I asked her.

Her answer came immediately. "Not Caleb. And please tell him that!" She looked me right in the eye, finally. "I don't owe anybody anything, anymore than you do, Nick." She smiled. "I hear you're getting out, too! I never thought you had the nerve! Congratulations!"

I didn't thank her. We left it at that.

I never saw her again after that June.

We read and heard about Unique, but not Jessie.

Art imitates life.

Due to a "shelfquake" caused by a strange cat, The Great Louse Hop was over before it began. Frankenlouse was spared the humiliation of not having a date, and he would never again be taunted as the hungry and horrible "onster." Just as my father had found Captain Tuttle's *Vietnam Journal*, due to Poison's panic, so did the man who owned *Frankenstein* find *it*, and take Frankenlouse back to the library where he really belonged.

CHAPTER THIRTY-FOUR

I was accepted by Music and Art.

On a hot summer night when my father was cutting up some sole for Poison in the kitchen, I asked him if we could talk about the coming year.

"You always want to have these serious talks when I'm doing something else," he said. "You should schedule such discussions so I can give them my full attention."

"Yes, sir. But I have to make my plans."

"What about my plans? I have my plans, too."

"What were you planning, sir?" I knew he didn't have any plans. It drove him crazy in the summer that he had all that unscheduled time on his hands.

"I have my reading," he said.

And indeed, he had on his eyeshade. He'd been reading until Poison started winding in and

out of his legs and purring. I'd seen him give in
to her, slap his newspaper down, get up and go
toward the kitchen while she ran after him.

Fanny was on vacation, like everyone else.

The two of us were "batching" it, but nothing
in our surroundings seemed that way. My father
prided himself on his ability to maintain order,
to keep to his self-imposed discipline, rising
at the same time every morning, keeping the
kitchen shipshape, jogging to the administration
building and back in time to make lunch for us.
He was tireless when it came to explaining to
me how to position plates, silverware, and
glasses in the dishwasher, and he could fold
sheets and pillowcases in a way you couldn't tell
from Fanny's style.

I thought of Caleb telling me his idea to raise
extra money had been to hire on as a jack-of-all-
trades summer helper in our home. He'd reminded me of my father's FFT saying a cadet
would always be welcome at Blister. Caleb had
said that after all he wasn't going to ask for a
free ride; he'd have been paying off his debt.
. . . He could never have passed my father's
inspection. I would look over my shoulder and
see The General redoing things I'd done: in the
kitchen, the bathroom, and outside at the garbage pails.

Now Caleb was in language camp somewhere in New Hampshire, sending postcards: one saying *"HELP!"* another *"¡SOCORRO!"* a third *"AU SECOURS!"*

I thought of my July Fourth visit to my mother's new apartment, where her belongings spilled out of the closets, and the bed was always unmade. Sam had taken us to a party aboard a houseboat on City Island, where we stood on deck in the starry night and watched the fireworks explode in the sky. . . . There were no schedules and no routine. My mother was freelancing. We went to midnight movies and had breakfast at noon. Sam took me to SoHo to show me where the real artists live and the best galleries were. I'd gotten used to him and to being stared at when I was with him. I liked the way he kept my mother laughing, even though Aunt Priscilla said it was really a form of mild hysteria because my mother didn't know how to get rid of him. . . . New York was the city of my dreams and I knew that I would always live there once I got there.

My father put the dish of sole on the floor and washed his hands.

I said, "I worry about Caleb."

"What's he done now?"

"I don't mean now. I mean next year."

"You're right to worry about him. I don't think he'll ever be a crow."

"You always say that."

"I think it's a safe thing to say."

"I worry about you, too, plowing around in this big house by yourself. Grandad won't even be nearby."

"I don't plow around."

"I take it back. You don't. You take every step very carefully, sir. . . . Still — it's a big house."

"Don't worry about us."

He meant Ike and him, and I had a suspicion he meant Poison, too. She spent most of her time resting languorously on his armchair, with Ike sleeping nearby, resigned to his place on the floor.

I said, "I'm not going to worry anymore. I do when I think about it, but I've made up my mind. I'm not going to anymore."

"Fine!" He dried his hands on a towel. "What do you have to talk about?"

"I want to talk about my not living here next year."

"What about it?"

"Do you know why I won't be here?"

"We've had this conversation, Nick."

"Not this one," I said. "Next year I won't be

here because I'd like to be in the barracks with Caleb and Kinya, if that's okay with you."

It took him a second to get my drift.

He frowned at me.

I said, "I want to keep my eye on Caleb. And if I was billeted over in Bradley with him, I could see this place from there, too."

"Did you change your mind or something?"

"Yes," I said. "Not about cartooning. Just about the timing. . . . I figure after Blister I can apply to a college that features art. Parsons or Cooper Union."

"West Point has art courses."

My father was a relentless man, sometimes a thankless man, or at least a man who could not voice a thank-you. But he was predictable, too, and it no longer bothered me that much that I would know what to expect, even in the way of rules.

For I *was* my father's son, in the long run, and not Unique's daughter, who may have been the one to change my mind that day she told me she didn't really care about rules, that Aaron was stupid or something, and that she didn't owe anyone anything, anymore than I did.

I figured that if she thought I didn't owe anyone anything, anymore than she did, then I probably did owe someone something.

That summer night while my father and I stood there watching Poison eat, I felt good about staying for two more years, becoming a crow, and graduating with my class.

Sometimes it was okay for one to follow two, for *A* to follow *B*, straight ahead . . . straight ahead.

Frankenlouse could wait, too, for me to make him famous. In the library where he'd been headed before he was loaned out, there was a large horror section with many others like him.

At first Spiderlouse, Dr. Jekyllouse, Tarantulalouse, Godzillalouse, and the other awesome and grotesque booklice were angry that because of this newcomer, there would be less *m*'s to relish.

But Frankenlouse made them a solemn promise which amazed them all, and endeared him to everyone.

He promised that he would never eat, look at, or even say the thirteenth letter of the alphabet.